Just then the whi[...]
workroom. The o[...]
and Chiun, who [...]
take no more.

"Hold!" he crie[...]

The slaves looked up, hope on their faces, expecting a deliverer. But all they saw was a small yellow man in a yellow robe, looking like a doll, whirling into the room, his eyes twisted in anger, glaring at the overseer.

The big man jumped down from his platform, whirled his whip over his head, and lashed it out at Chiun.

Like a meat slicer, Chiun's right hand moved up alongside his head and, as the whip reached him, he sliced off a neat six inches with the side of his palm.

The overseer drew back the whip, readying an overhead slash that would slice a man's shoulder down to the bone. He released it with full power, but the lash stopped at Chiun. The overseer tried to let go of the whip, but it was attached to his right wrist with a thong. The small Oriental was pulling him across the floor. As he was being dragged, he pulled out his pistol.

He never had time to pull the trigger. An almost-gentle-appearing blow from Chiun's index finger pushed his lower mandible back into his spinal column with a total, terminal snap.

THE DESTROYER SERIES

The Destroyer

CHAINED REACTION #34

by Richard Sapir & Warren Murphy

PINNACLE BOOKS • LOS ANGELES

This is a work of fiction. All the characters and events portrayed in this book are fictional, and any resemblance to real people or incidents is purely coincidental.

DESTROYER #34: CHAINED REACTION

An original Pinnacle Books edition, published for the first time anywhere.

First printing, September 1978

ISBN: 0-523-40156-6

Cover illustration by Hector Garrido

Printed in the United States of America

PINNACLE BOOKS, INC.
2029 Century Park East
Los Angeles, California 90067

For Art and Sue Cloutier,
and the Williamses: John,
Betty, Christina, Felicia, and Jennifer
—D.S.

An Apology to the Readers

"From time to time there has appeared an American post office box in the front of these books. Many people, appreciating the glory and wisdom of Sinanju, wrote to that address hoping to be enlightened. Many of those letters were unanswered because Sapir and Murphy were in charge of my answers. Those letters will remain unanswered because of the sloth of Sapir and Murphy, now rich men because of my greatness. I, Master of the House of Sinanju, apologize for the cheap white help."

By his august hand this 177th day of the Year of Dread Wind, 4,875, we are:
—Chiun

"I was answering the letters when Sapir said he didn't like the way I was doing it and would take it over. Since then, your letters have been unanswered."
—W. B. Murphy

"Murphy has known me almost twenty years. Anyone who has known me that long had to know I wouldn't answer the letters.

But that's typical of Murphy—a victim of hope surmounting awesome evidence. All I said to him was that he was doing a lousy job and that I could do better. In any case, most of the letters were for Chiun. I am hiring a new bookkeeper. If I can find the letters, I may answer them. But since it is only a moral and spiritual obligation, don't get your hopes up. I think I forgot to keep up payments on the post office box. However, I did keep them up for many years, but not one of you thought to write me and say 'good job.' "

—R. Sapir

CHAINED REACTION

CHAPTER ONE

Walker Teasdale III knew he was going to die, knew he had less than a week to live, and knew it made no sense to plan on anything, even his next meal.

He fell into a steady gloom with a vacant stare that no one in Bravo Company could break or even enter.

"Walker, do you know what you're doin', boy? You're gonna get this whole outfit bad marks. That's what you're gonna do, boy," threatened another recruit in the bunk next to his.

Walker was nineteen years old, with sandy hair, a bony build, and a face waiting for manhood to line it with years. His light blue eyes, like empty Caribbean pools, stared nowhere. He rested his chin on his M-16 and answered the intruder from his vision of gloom.

"Ah don' care what happens to the outfit. Ah don' care what happens to anybody. Ah don' care anymore. Ah'm gonna die and that's that."

"How you know you're gonna die, boy?" asked the other recruit, who always seemed to know more than Walker. He was from the big city, Charleston.

Walker had been to Charleston, South Carolina,

only twice, once to sell a funny rock he had found to a university feller who was supposed to pay a good price for such things. It was a real good price too, $15.35, and Walker trudged nineteen miles each way to get that price. The second time he had been to Charleston had been to enlist in this special unit that paid for everything and gave you everything.

The other recruits knew Walker was "real country" because he liked the food. Walker thought chipped beef on toast was a treat for months until the other recruits teased him out of it. But he still went back for seconds and ate the leftover portions. He just didn't smack his lips as much anymore. That was all.

Walker cried at Gene Autry movies when the other recruits booed because the show was in black and white.

Walker prayed before he went to bed.

Walker did his calisthenics even when the drill sergeant's white stick wasn't there to prod.

Walker carried the packs of others on forced thirty-mile hikes.

Walker turned himself in for falling asleep on duty.

Walker cried when "Dixie" was played. When the national anthem was played. When Geritol commercials came on television, because it was "so nice to see people in love at such an old age." The old age, for Walker, was thirty-four.

So they laughed at him because he was country. But no one laughed at the rifle range. Walker became the unit sniper in the first two weeks. While other recruits from Chicago and Santa Fe were being told to put the little needle at the front of the barrel between the little V at the back of the barrel and sight the whole thing just under the target, Walker was drilling bull's-eyes. A Walker Teasdale target looked as if someone had taken a rock and pressed out the center.

Walker said there was no secret.

"You jes' put 'er in there real easy, is all."

"But how?" he was asked.

"You jes' do it," Walker replied and he was never able to teach the other recruits how to put out a buzzard's eye, as he called the center of the target.

Everyone teased Walker.

When he asked why the basic training of this outfit was almost two full years, he was told it was that way because he held everyone back.

When he asked where "the nigras" were, they told Walker that a big bear in the hills ate them all up and then everyone rolled on the barracks floor in laughter.

But that question did get some people thinking. Where were the blacks?

"They ain't smart enough to get into this outfit," said the recruit from Chicago.

"There are some smart niggers," said the recruit from Sante Fe. "They got to have a few. This is the army, isn't it?"

And then the recruits started remembering the strange requirements and questions when they enlisted. Half the questions seemed to be about blacks and how the recruits felt about them.

One said he thought he hadn't stood a chance of getting into the outfit when he answered, "The only good one is a dead one. A dead nigger won't

3

mug you, won't welfare off you, won't mess up your neighborhood. Only thing niggers ever do good in the world is fertilize. And if they had any choice about that, they wouldn't do that either."

"You said that?" asked Walker Teasdale, unbelieving.

"Yessir," said the other recruit.

"Gollee," Walker Teasdale had said. "Ah thought it was against the law not to like nigras."

"Ah hate 'em," said the other recruit.

"Seems a waste of time to hate anybody," said Walker.

"Not niggers. Any time you spend hating them is time well spent."

"Well, ah don't hate nobody," said Walker. "There's good and bad in all kinds."

"Ceppin' niggers is mostly bad," laughed the other recruit, and training became so hard, with the constant repetition of tiring drills, that the strangeness of the unit became less a topic of discussion than survival in the following few days.

There were drills like silence. Five men would be told a secret by the commanding officer and then sent out into the field. This secret would not be mentioned again until two weeks later when the five were brought before the commanding officer, Lt. Colonel Wendell Bleech, a rotund, pink-faced ball of a man with a harsh crew cut and extra large epaulettes on his shoulders, which let the cloth of his military blouse hang fuller over his suet-bloated body.

Colonel Bleech liked to talk about mean and lean. Colonel Bleech liked toasted English muffins with peach jam and sweet butter.

4

Colonel Bleech also liked to punish in front of the assembled unit. He went beyond enlightened rehabilitation. He broke noses and arms and legs and threatened each time, "the next time I get rough."

Colonel Bleech had a riding crop with lead balls laced into the flattened pommel. Colonel Bleech pointed to two of the recruits.

"The secrets I told you are no longer secrets. They have come back to me. I swore you to secrecy. Do you know the most important thing in a man's makeup and character is his word? You have violated your word. You have raped your word. You have desecrated your word. Now what do you two have to say for it?"

They said they were sorry.

"Now, see, men, I have a problem," said Bleech. He liked high riding boots and balloon riding pants. He looked like a tan pumpkin. Anyone who hadn't seen him kick prostrate recruits in the groin would think he was downright cherubic. He slapped his crop against his shiny riding boots.

"I have a real serious problem, men, because I would like to believe you. I would like to believe you are sorry. I am a believing man. But I have discovered that you are liars. That you give your word and it is meaningless. Is that correct?"

"Yessir," answered the two recruits, at stiff attention, their eyes sneaking glances at the flicking crop, snapping every so often against the hard leather boots.

"Being unable to take your word that you will be sorry, I must make sure."

The crop snapped against a nose. The young

man covered the bloody streak across his face with his hands. He gasped. His eyes teared.

Little drops of blood came down his nasal passage to the rear of his throat. He tasted it, hot and choking.

"Now I know you're sorry," said Bleech. "I know you are truly and deeply sorry. That's how I have to do things when I can't take a man's word."

And with that, he snapped a knee into the groin of the second recruit and that boy went over in two, his face coming very close to the ground very quickly. He opened his mouth to scream a silent scream. And Bleech stepped on the back of his head, pushing his face into the ground, then ground the polished heel of the polished boot into the boy's jaw, where a sickening crack happened and the boot sank two inches into the face and the jaw was broken.

"That's for talkers, boys. But this is nothing compared to what will happen if you talk outside. There is no greater sin in this man's world than talking outside the unit."

Colonel Bleech stomped a polished foot in the South Carolina dust. It was a hot dry summer in these hills of the training camp, where no paved roads led and the only entrance the recruits knew about was by helicopter.

Lordy, did they know helicopters. They knew loading and unloading the way most people knew how to swallow. They knew how to carry people, both willing and reluctant. They had more techniques for dragging someone by lip or ear or even chain than they could count.

Only one person never questioned an order of

the peculiarity of the training. And that was the big raw-boned boy from near Pieraffle, South Carolina, twenty-seven miles south of Charleston, the boy who liked Gene Autry movies, chipped beef on toast, who never got tired, and who spoke kindly about Lt. Colonel Wendell Bleech, even behind his back.

So when Walker Teasdale fell into despondency, his chin resting on the barrel of his rifle, his eyes looking into that great nowhere where people see no tomorrow, the other recruits took special notice.

"How do you know you're going to get killed, Walker?" they asked.

"I know. I know how, too," he said. "They're gonna shoot me for disciplinary reasons. I know it. They're gonna take me out to that piney hill and they're gonna make me dig my grave and then they're gonna put a bullet in my head."

"Who's they, Walker?"

"Colonel Bleech and the drill sergeants."

"You? They think you're perfect."

"They won't tomorrow."

"Nobody knows what's going to happen tomorrow, Walker."

"I do," said Walker, firm in gaze and voice, a steady sureness in his manner, as when he talked about putting bullets into targets.

He asked for a glass of water and young men who ordinarily wouldn't wait on anyone unless ordered by a superior jumped to find a glass. There were no glasses in the barracks, so someone drank the last bit of smuggled moonshine in a mason jar, washed it out with water, and filled it.

Walker put his gun on his rack and, with a slow

7

wisdom that had replaced his boyish innocence, looked at the water, then drank it all.

"This is my last sustenance, fellas. Ah've seen the buzzards in my dreams and they called my name. Ah take no more food or drink."

The other recruits thought this was pretty much craziness, since no one had seen a buzzard around these parts since coming to camp more than ten months ago, all of them thinking that basic training should have been a two-month affair and finding out, in an address by Colonel Bleech, that two months wasn't enough to teach a man to tie his shoes right, let alone become a soldier, a real soldier.

When Bleech said "soldier," his voice lowered, his spine stiffened, and a deep pride came to his entire bearing. His lead-weighted riding crop would always tap at his polished boots on that word.

On the morning that Walker Teasdale said he would die, the recruits were awakened as usual with drill sergeants screaming in their ears, for their usual semiclothed morning run, wearing just boots, shorts, and rifles with full packs of ammunition.

Long ago, they had stopped commenting on how none of them had ever heard of basic training like this, with a five-mile run every morning and at triple time. One of the recruits who had a brother in the Airborne once tried to chant as he ran and had to run punishment miles because this unit never made noise when it ran, when it fought, and when it marched.

"There'll be plenty of noise on the great day," Colonel Bleech had promised, but everyone was

8

afraid to ask what that great day was, although they had heard a lieutenant mention it, too, but the lieutenant admitted he didn't know what that great day was. All he knew was that he owned two homes, an Alfa Romeo sports car, and sent his two daughters to private schools—all on a lieutenant's pay.

The pay was good, but tired, frightened young men do not think of money when they want only rest. And they don't think of money when they are thinking only of dying.

Walker Teasdale did his five-mile run with the unit that morning and passed up his favorite chipped beef on toast, even though the other recruits kept passing him heaping portions of it.

They packed for a two-day marching into what was called Watts City, a specially constructed battle site in which the unit maneuvered through alleys and simulated taverns and empty lots. Whoever built Watts City, someone said, must have cheated on the contract because the whole thing looked like a slum.

As they double-timed through piney woods, their bodies now hardened and moving easily without complaint of lung or muscle, dark birds circled and pivoted in the delicate blue sky.

"Buzzards," whispered someone and everyone looked to Walker and then the birds. Only one trooper that day refused to look up. He knew the birds would be there. He had dreamed them. He had seen them in his sleep as he had seen this piney hill. And he knew his time was coming.

They marched as the sun made their uniforms sweat-wet clinging clothes. The pine needles, soft beneath their feet, had at one time made bloody

9

blisters, but now these blisters were callouses. The recruits hardly noticed the tax levied on their bodies by the march.

Most thought they were on another mock raid on Watts City, but at the outskirts of the reconstructed slum they turned away and double-timed down into a leafy valley with a small brown mudwater stream, and there Walker Teasdale saw the little hill above him that he had seen in his dream.

And if he had not been staring at that hill, he might not have seen the brown boot stick out from behind a tree. Other recruits rested, but Walker stared at the hill. He knew he would have all the rest he would ever need, soon and forever.

The other recruits took their smoking break by the muddy stream. And then a bugle seemed to come out of the sky and they all looked up but saw nothing. Only Walker saw the slender object in the hand of Colonel Bleech atop the small piney hill.

It sounded like the voice of God coming from all the trees, but Walker knew the small object must be a microphone and the voice was Colonel Bleech's and was coming from hidden speakers in the trees.

"The greatest violation that can ever occur has occurred," came the voice from the hills and sky and even the stream. It was around them and in them.

But only innocent Walker knew what the voice was.

"Treason. Rank and utter treason has occurred and the party is over. I tried to be understanding with you. Reasonable with you. Moderate with you. And what do I get in return? Treason."

"That's Bleech, isn't it?" whispered one recruit.

"Shhhh. Maybe he can hear," said another.

"Where is he anyway?"

"Shhhh. You wanna make it worse?"

"Treason," came the colonel's voice. "Pay attention while you hear the insidious ingratitude of one of you. No more kid gloves. No more kindergarten wrist-slapping. Treason calls for death and one of you will die today for this infamy. If only I had exercised discipline before," said Bleech to his unit, most of whose members had scars from his "little reminders" as he liked to call the punches and kicks and crop whips, "I wouldn't have to exercise this ultimate discipline now. You can blame me, men. If I had been firm before, one of you wouldn't have to die now."

The recruits all looked to Walker Teasdale who was still standing up, leaning on his rifle.

Atop the hill, Colonel Bleech took a toasted English muffin from his orderly, who had crawled with it so as not to be seen by the recruits down in the little valley across the muddy stream. The colonel thought it would have been highly unmilitary, when staging a punishment, to be seen receiving a toasted English muffin with sweet butter and jam. So he ordered the young aide to crawl to him.

Bleech saw the terrified young men below him waiting on his words. It was good to hang them out like this, make each one think, if possible, that he was the one going to be executed. Bleech knew full well that you executed people, not so

11

much of because of what they had done, but because of what you didn't want the survivors to do.

What the young recruits did not know was that for every nose broken, every groin shattered, there had been a plan.

Those with permanent damage were scheduled for inside work, after the "great day" came. But Colonel Bleech never broke a limb or caused permanent damage to anyone on his combat squads. He disguised this cunning with feigned rage. Nothing like being angry to hide the fact that you were a thinking man.

"Treason," boomed Bleech, taking a buttery bite from the muffin. His orderly was on the ground and a drop of melted butter landed on his forehead. Bleech dismissed the man who crawled back down the far side of the hill. Bleech let the word "treason" hang out above the valley below as he finished the muffin, licking the sweet red jam from his lips. It was a British jam and he didn't like British jams. Not enough sugar or tartness. The whole thing tasted like dental cement.

Bleech slipped his notes from his neatly pressed shirt pocket. "We have all been betrayed. And not just to the Russians or the Chinese. No . . . worse. We were betrayed to those who can do us the most damage, who can destroy everything we have worked and trained for. Treason."

Bleech sensed he wasn't reaching the men and from many years of correctly judging these things, he knew his senses could be trusted. They should have been looking nervously at each other, but instead all were staring now at one recruit, the one recruit who could not possibly have violated the code of honor of the unit.

They were looking at Walker Teasdale and Bleech could not understand why. Teasdale had only one fault—he wasn't mean enough. But other than that, he would be the last person to violate an oath of secrecy.

Colonel Bleech did not like things happening by accident and down there, among his seven hundred men, something was happening that he had not planned. He had planned his training and perfected it and now he had a unit he would take into the bowels of hell and would not lose a single man needlessly. He knew what they thought and what they did and their staring at Teasdale annoyed him.

Bleech continued his harangue but watched the men spread out in the valley below.

"Here is the treason. Here is a letter we intercepted. It reads like this:

" 'Dear Sir. More than a year ago I signed up with a special unit of the army. It offered extra pay, extra benefits, and a cash bonus of three thousand dollars for my enlistment. Instead of the usual basic training, we have been in training for ten months. The officers strike us at will. We cannot communicate with our families. Half the training is teaching us how to whip people and chain people. Now, I know this is not the regular army. For one thing, there's no paperwork, hardly. And another thing is there are no negroes in the outfit and we watch movies about how bad they are and how wonderful the old South used to be. What I want to know is this army regulation and how can I get out of it. I hate it.' "

Bleech paused. And then he knew what he would do. He would seize the surprise and make it his own. If they thought Walker Teasdale was the culprit, let them. It would be more of a surprise. But this time it would be his surprise.

"Teasdale, come up the hill," he bellowed.

The young raw-boned boy moved slowly, his feet leaden with a sudden tiredness of a body unwilling to go to its end.

"Move. Double time, Teasdale," said Bleech into the microphone.

When he was close, Colonel Bleech switched off the microphone and said in a hushed voice, "Teasdale, come here. I'm behind the tree."

"I know, sir. I saw you."

"Walker, it's not you. Don't look so ashen-faced, son. You did not write this letter. You never would. I know that."

"It's my day to die, Colonel."

"Nonsense. You're going to be the one doing the executing. We'll play a little joke on the boys, eh?"

"It's my day to die, sir."

"Have you told *them* that?" asked Bleech, his fat crewcutted head nodding down toward the little valley.

"Yessir."

"That explains it. Don't worry. You're going to live. You're one of my best men and my best men live because I want them to live. We need good men."

"Yessir," said Teasdale, but his voice was still heavy.

Colonel Bleech switched on the microphone.

"Now, there is a trooper sitting on a rock, by

14

the stream, hiding himself away from me. Come up here. No, not you. The one looking away from me. Drake. You, Drake. Trooper Anderson Drake. Get up here."

Walker Teasdale knew Drake. He had complained a lot, said he was going to do something about it, and a few weeks ago stopped complaining. Drake had been saying he had never heard of an outfit like this. Drake had been saying the outfit must be illegal. Teasdale thought he was lucky to be in an outfit that was unlike any other because that meant it was special. Teasdale was proud to be part of a special unit. That's why he had joined.

And the bonus also paid for another four acres of rich bottom land, which was cheap back home in Jefferson County because the roads were so bad you couldn't get your harvest to market. Teasdale gave the money to the family, all but five dollars of it, with which he bought a shiny red box of chocolate candies at the big store in Nawl's Hollow and gave that to his girl who put it away for later, although Walker was sort of hoping she would open it then, but he rightly couldn't blame her because when they had become engaged and he had gotten her a similar box, he had eaten most of them, and all the cream-filled ones.

He watched Drake make it up the hill stumbling more than ordinarily, and Teasdale, knowing Drake was clumsy on obstacle courses, came to the conclusion that those who did badly at their soldiering were also most likely to be those who violated the rules the most. Walker lumped this together as some sort of contagious badness

15

within the person, spilling over from bad work to bad conduct.

Drake, a red-haired boy from Altoona, Pennsylvania, who tended to sunburn easily, had a crimson face by the time he got close.

"Trooper Drake reporting, sir," he said when he saw Colonel Bleech step out from behind the tree. "Sir, I'm innocent, sir."

"I have the letter, Drake."

"Sir, may I explain?"

"Shhhh," said Colonel Bleech. "About face. Look at the men."

"Sir, I had help from other troopers. I'll give you their names."

"I don't want their names. I know everyone involved. I know everything in this unit. We have people everywhere and they all look out for us. Know this. Your commanding officer knows everything."

And Bleech winked to Teasdale as Drake turned around. Walker Teasdale heard something rustling behind him and there, crawling up from a jeep with a long curved sword, was the colonel's orderly. He held the sword curved in his hands as his elbows dug into the loamy pine-needled earth, and Teasdale realized that those down below would only see Drake and him, and would not see the colonel and the aide.

Walker Teasdale had seen the colonel behind the tree only because he had recognized the place he was going to die.

Bleech motioned Teasdale behind the tree. He winked and put a friendly arm around Teasdale's shoulders. Walker didn't know whether to be more surprised by the friendly arm or the sword.

16

They had practiced twice against melons but everyone thought it was a joke. Nobody used swords nowadays.

"Give me a nice clean cut, Walker," whispered Bleech, pointing to Drake's neck. "I want the head to roll. If it doesn't roll, son, kick it down the hill."

Walker stared at Drake's neck and saw the little hairs growing over the edge of his collar. He felt the hard wood handle of the sword and noticed that the blade had burnished edges. It had been sharpened recently. It was heavy in his hands and his palms became moist and he did not want to lift the sword.

"At the neck," said Bleech. "A nice even stroke. Come on, boy."

Teasdale felt the air become hot in his lungs and leadenness draped his body, like chains holding him down. His stomach became watery like a cheap pancake syrup and he did not move.

"Walker, do it," said Bleech, loud enough for the tone of the order to get through.

Drake turned his head and, seeing the sword in Teasdale's hands, covered his face. His body trembled like a spring on the end of a jerking string and a dark brown spot spread on his pants, as he released his bladder out of fear.

"Teasdale," shouted Bleech and, losing his temper, he depressed the switch on the microphone in his hand and the entire unit heard their commanding officer yell, "Trooper Walker Teasdale, you cut off that head now. Clean and fast. Now."

Down in the valley, it sounded like the voice of the heavens and then the whole unit noticed who

17

was up there with Drake and Teasdale. It was the colonel and he was giving an order and ol' Walker Teasdale wasn't doing anything about it. Why, he wanted Walker to cut off Drake's head, for treason. It wasn't Teasdale's time to die at all, but Trooper Drake's.

Bleech caught all this in an instant.

"I am giving you a direct order," said Bleech and then, flipping off the microphone, added, "They've all seen and heard my order. It's too late now, son. You've got to take Drake's head. Now, c'mon. You'll be happy afterwards."

Walker tightened his grip on the sword. The aide crawled away. Walker raised the sword high as he had been taught because you could not take a head swinging just any which-way; you took it level because the blade had to cleave through the vertebrae level or it got jammed in bone. That's what the instructor had said.

He pulled back the sword. He planted his left foot and then Drake looked around. He looked at Teasdale's eyes and stared, and Teasdale prayed that Drake would just turn away. It was hard enough knowing the man, but killing him when he was looking in Teasdale's eyes? Walker couldn't do it. He had sworn to kill enemies, not people he knew.

"Please," said Teasdale. "Please turn your head away."

"Okay," said Drake, softly, as if Walker had asked him to remove his hat or something.

And the way he said it, so pleasant and meek, Teasdale knew it was all over. He let the sword drop from his hand.

"I'm sorry, Colonel. I'll kill an enemy but I can't kill one of our own men."

"I can't allow the unit to trust each other against my orders, Teasdale. This is my last warning. You've got to do it."

And then the microphone was on again as though the trees down below were breathing static and Colonel Bleech gave his last order to Trooper Walker Teasdale.

"Cut off his head."

"No," said Teasdale.

"Drake," said Bleech. "Do you follow orders?"

"Yessir."

"If I let you live, will you follow orders?"

"Oh, yessir. Yessir. Yessir. Anything. Special unit all the way."

"I'm going to get a head one way or another. Drake. Give me Teasdale's head."

Trooper Drake, still trembling with fear, dove for the sword, lest Teasdale change his mind. He snapped it from the rawboned young man's hands and was up and swinging wildly in an instant. He took a slash at the head and the blade cut through flesh and bounced back off the skull, stunning Teasdale. He felt the blade crack at his head again and then he heard his colonel talking about a level blow from behind and there was a stinging at the back of his head and then a deep dark numbness.

The eyes did not see as his head bounced down the hill rolling crazily in bumps and bounces like a punted football making its way toward an end zone.

The eyes did not see, nor did the ears hear. The

19

body was back up on the hill spurting red rivers from the neck.

But a last thought was held somewhere out in the vastness of a universe that went on forever.

And that thought was that Colonel Bleech, for all his talk of soldiering and killing, was but a clumsy amateur at best. And by this evil deed he had offended a power in the center of the universe, a power so vast it would unleash the ultimate force of man.

And when that force was unleashed, Bleech would be but a pitiful popped pumpkin, splattered like the melons the men had practiced their sword thrusts on.

CHAPTER TWO

His name was Remo and it was his last assignment. He did not know the man, but he never knew the men. He knew their names and what they looked like and where he could find them.

But he no longer cared about what they had done or why they had done it. He cared only that when he finished them it was neat and clean and with an economy of motion.

This last man lived in the penthouse of a hotel in Miami Beach. There were only three entrances to it, all guarded, all locked with triple keys that three men had to agree to use simultaneously, and since a former security advisor to the Central Intelligence Agency had designed this little hotel fortress and guaranteed it impenetrable from above or below, the man slept that morning with ease and contentment, until Remo grabbed his fleshy pink face in his hands and said into the stunned eyes that he would squeeze the man's cheeks off unless he explained some things very quickly.

Remo knew the man's shock was not at his appearance. Remo was a moderately handsome man with high cheekbones and a dark stare that tended to liquefy the resolve of women when he turned it on them, if he cared about that anymore, which he didn't. He was thin, lean to perfection, and only his thick wrists might indicate that this man might be anything different from normal.

The assignment certainly wasn't. Remo had seen this sort of penthouse arrangement fourteen times. He called it "the sandwich." They put a nice piece of bread on top with perhaps a machine gun or two, several men and a metal shield reinforcing the roof, and they locked all the entrances below, probably adding devices there, and so the top and bottom were nice and cozy and safe. But the middle was as open as a French bikini.

The attack on it was not new with Remo; it had not been new fifty years ago or fifteen hundred, for that matter.

Remo had been told about the first successful assault on the fortress defense.

To protect themselves against assassins, ancient kings would take the highest floors for their sleeping quarters, put their most trusted men below and above and go to sleep in the illusion of safety.

This problem occurred to a Master of Sinanju in A.D. 427 (by western dating) when a Himalayan prince put his brothers as guards above and below him, and arranged it so that his son hated the prince's brothers, so that the brothers knew that if the prince died, his son would become prince and slaughter them all. This was known to the Master of Sinanju, the reigning assassin in an ages-old house of assassins whose labors went to support a tiny village in cold bleak North Korea.

The Master knew that people worked with their fears instead of their minds. Because they were afraid of heights, they thought others would be. Because they slipped on smooth stone walls, they thought others would. Because they moved with noise, they thought others did and their ears would be protection.

The fortress sandwich was always open in the middle and that Master of Sinanju had taken less than a minute to realize he had only to move up the wall and enter at the level of the prince's room to complete his duty, and thus win that year, as it was written in the records of Sinanju, food and grain for ten years from a grateful enemy prince. Also a bust of that king, which Remo had once seen stored in that peculiar domicile in the village of Sinanju, a town he did not intend to return to ever again no matter how many generations of master assassins it had produced, none of whom had ever given one more minute of thought to wondering about how to penetrate the fortress defense.

And Remo didn't either.

He found the hotel and didn't even bother to look up.

Hastings Vining, one of the major commodities brokers, owned the hotel and lived in the top two floors. Remo didn't even bother to figure out whether he was sleeping in the twenty-third or twenty-fourth floor. It was the twenty-fourth. It was always the highest floor.

People always equated height with safety and assumed that people would first try to enter from below or then from above. They worried about helicopters and parachutes and even balloons, but they never gave a thought to somebody who could just climb up the smooth walls of a building.

Remo didn't feel like working that hard that morning so he took an elevator to the twenty-second floor and knocked on a door.

"Who is it?" called out a woman's voice.

"Gas man. Problem with hotel gas. Got to fix it."

"Problem with gas? This hotel doesn't have gas. I don't have gas. Try the kitchen."

"You've got gas now, lady, and it might be dangerous. I've got to go outside and check your gas."

"Are you from the hotel?"

"Check the desk, lady," said Remo with that sort of bored surliness that for some peculiar reason bred trust in most people.

"Oh, all right," said the woman and the door opened. She was in her early fifties and her face glistened with creams fighting their losing battle in a retreating action from youth, whose only victory was not getting worse for another day. She wore a floppy pink muumuu and had her hair in some sort of plastic device.

"Anything you want," she said with a lewd grin when she saw Remo.

She was suddenly awake and happy. She adjusted one pink device in her reddish hair and smiled again. This time she licked her lips invitingly. Remo wondered how much creamy gook got attached to her tongue when she did that.

"Just the gas, lady."

"I want you and I'll pay you for it," she said.

"All right," said Remo, who knew never to argue with someone obsessed. "Tonight."

"Now," she said.

"Lunch," said Remo.

"Breakfast."

"Danish snack," he said, seeing the years of pastry in the woman's face and assuming it meant 10 A.M.

"Not now?" she whined.

"Got to check the gas," he said. He would be out way before 10 A.M. He would be out of the whole thing in ten minutes and out of this career in thirty.

He gave her a wink. She winked back and her eyelashes stuck together and she had to dislodge them manually.

Remo moved through the suite's entertaining room with his normal silence. He hadn't thought about moving like this for more than ten years. The silence came from the breathing rhythms and the body in unity with its nervous system and its own internal rhythms. All things had rhythms, most too subtle to be perceived by those untrained and not even suspected by those who clogged their systems with meat fats and took bare little jerky breaths, hardly ever washing the full lung with oxygen as they should.

Remo only noticed he was moving correctly when the woman gasped, "My god. You move like a ghost. You don't make sounds."

"It's your ears," lied Remo and he was out the window, onto the ledge, and then pressed against the brick, salty with the Miami Beach sea air, and somewhat worn by cars' exhaust fumes. The wear was not much but the brick edges became crumbly and one had to be extra careful not to rely on them. Instead he had to bring the wall

25

into himself and press upward. A full ledge could be used for a leap, but there was no ledge beneath his feet now, and the wall had to be worked meticulously.

"How are you doing that? What are you standing on?" It was the woman. Her head out the window. She was eye-level with his feet.

"It's a trick. See you later, sweetheart."

"How do you do that?"

"Mind control," Remo said. "I've got tremendous mental discipline."

"Can I do that?"

"Sure. Later."

"It looks so easy. Like you're doing nothing. You're just moving up the wall," said the woman, her voice rising in amazement as she turned her head to follow the progress of the attractive young man.

There it was. She was sure of it. The feet were touching nothing. They were pressed into the wall itself and it was like he was creating a suction force with his body. But where was the suction?

She imagined herself between that man and the wall and this so aroused her that she momentarily thought of flinging herself out the window and making him catch her. But what if he wouldn't catch her? She looked down. It was a long way down and the surf looked so small below, like pieces of Christmas tree tinsel floating in a huge wide blue-green bathtub. And right near the beach, those two heart-shaped green swimming pools for those who preferred chlorine to salt.

She pulled in her head.

Remo moved up to the twenty-third floor, caught a ledge with his right hand, and yanked, so that when he went up and by with only a little tap from his foot, he was hanging onto the ledge of the twenty-fourth floor. With a slight swaying, he got his body into a pendulum motion, released at the top of the arc, and was one window over, so he went window flip to window flip until he reached the largest window at the corner, wedged it open, and surprise, surprise, here was the master bedroom.

Hastings Vining had assumed the outside was safest because he could get more layers of protection between himself and the doors below. They always took an outside room and, as befitted the station of whatever kind of lord they might happen to be, the largest room. So Remo was in the room and he awakened the man by squeezing his cheeks.

"Hold on," said Remo, holding the face in his right hand, while he searched his black chino slacks for the note. He had written down what he was supposed to ask.

"Just a minute, we've got it right here," said Remo. He felt that swelling strain of the man's jaw just before it cracked—bone did that before it broke—and he eased the grip but not enough to let the face out of it.

"I've got it. I've got it," said Remo. He recognized his own handwriting.

"All right. One fattened duck, curry powder, brown rice, half a pound . . . oops. Sorry. Shopping. Just a minute. I really do have it. I took it down this morning. Hold on. Here it is." Remo cleared his throat. "All righty, who are your government contacts on the Russian grain deal? How much did you pay them? When did you pay them and what are your current plans with the grain futures? Yeah. That's right," said Remo and he allowed the jaw to move. But the lips started to cry out for help and Remo had to grab the jaw again. He also sent an excruciating pain through the left ear with the forefingers of his left hand as he held the paper in his mouth. It was wet but he managed again.

This time he got answers. He got names. He got amounts. He got numbers of bank accounts in which the money was deposited. He got everything.

"One more thing," asked Remo.

Hastings Vining nodded in absolute terror. He had been sleeping and then suddenly there was someone tearing his face off. And he couldn't call his guards. He couldn't do anything but say whatever the man wanted to stop the pain.

So Hastings Vining, one of the leading commodities brokers in the world, babbled out everything the man wanted and held back nothing. When he said he wanted one more thing, Vining nodded. He had given the most incriminating evidence against himself he possibly could. Nothing else could harm him more.

"A pencil," said Remo. "I want a pencil. And could you repeat everything slowly?"

"I don't have a pencil," said Vining. "I don't. I honestly don't. I swear I don't."

"Have a pen?"

"No. I have a dictating machine."

"I don't trust machines," said Remo.

"I have a pen outside. In the vestibule. But Big Jack's there. He's my bodyguard. He's out there."

"That's all right," said Remo. He should have brought a pencil. This always happened. When you needed a pencil you never had one, yet when you didn't need one they were rolling around everywhere.

"You don't mind my bodyguard bringing a pen?"

"Not at all," said Remo. "But it better write."

Trembling, Vining rose from the bed and took hesitant barefoot steps across the deep white carpet of the master bedroom of his penthouse fortress. He opened a large double door a crack and put his face outside where the intruder could not see. Big Jack was dozing.

"Jack," said Vining and Big Jack opened his eyes, startled.

"I'm sorry, Mr. Vining," apologized Big Jack for sleeping on the job.

"Jack, I want a pen," said Vining and tried to move his eyes in such a way as to indicate there was someone else in the room with him.

Big Jack looked puzzled. He squinted his gross face and rubbed an eyebrow. He offered a pen he had been doodling with on a magazine. He liked to draw pictures of breasts. Big Jack would hide them when people came round, but he lined his magazines with ballpoint drawings of breasts. He had once told a friend there were thirty-seven different kinds of nipples. That was the other thing Big Jack knew. The first was breaking heads. He had done that for a loan shark in Jersey City until Mr. Vining had given him this respectable job and now he only broke heads in self defense if anyone tried to get physical with Mr. Vining. This had not happened for two years.

"The other pen," said Vining and Big Jack understood it was time for his gun. He had never used it for Mr. Vining before but he was going to use it now. All his life, he had been a victim of insidious bigotry. People thought that when you were six-foot-six and two hundred and eighty pounds, you didn't have the delicacy or the skill to shoot a gun. And that was prejudice. Because Big Jack could shoot a gun real good. He had put two holes side-by-side in the chest of Willie Ganetti back in Jersey City in '69. And he got James Trothman, a lawyer who wanted to squeal on a client, with a very precise shot under the left ear and at a good distance too. Yet this prejudice against big men persisted and Mr. Vining had never asked him to use his .45 automatic before.

And when his big hand went beneath his coat and Mr. Vining nodded very slowly and said very distinctly, "Yes, that's the pen I mean," it was, for Big Jack, John F. Kennedy becoming the first Catholic President of the United States, Jackie Robinson becoming the first black to play in the major leagues, and the Israelis winning the first Jewish war in two thousand years.

Big Jack was going to use his gun. He was out of the arm-breaking, nose-busting, kick-'em-in-the-butt, throw-'em-against-the-wall league of musclemen.

He had been called upon, by Hastings Vining himself, to kill with the gun. Tears of joy filled his eyes.

The .45, a large handgun for almost anyone,

looked like a toy pistol in the hairy, massive right mitt of Big Jack.

Hastings Vining, seeing his large bodyguard rise so quickly and happily to the occasion, suddenly wanted to call him off. This was death coming at him and death, even when under his command, set him aback. He knew the swindles of percentages and how to negotiate with federal prosecutors. He could maneuver a man into a corner so he owned him. He could play a drought in the Ukraine against the price of fertilizer in Des Moines, Iowa. He could see in a man's eyes the difference between 7 percent on a deal and 7.5.

But Hastings Vining could not stomach blood and for an instant he wanted to tell Big Jack, who always made him nervous anyhow, just being around, to go back to sleep.

It was too late. The hulk held his gun behind his back and came into the room. Vining stepped back and let his bodyguard past, then, for the first time since the horror of waking up with his face being ripped off, he felt some control of the situation. Now he was planning which prosecutor would handle the killing, which lawyer would defend Big Jack, and exactly how long Big Jack would have to be with the courts until they ruled, as they must rule, that Big Jack had killed in justifiable homicide. Also there was the question of bonus for Big Jack, not too big so that he would tend to litter the penthouse with bodies, but enough so that he would know that killing in defense of the precious life of Hastings Vining was highly approved.

"I wanted a pen, not a weapon," said the intruder.

Now, how could he see that, thought Vining. The chrome-plated pistol was still behind the bodyguard's back. The intruder had never seen the gun. Was it possible, wondered Vining, that Big Jack had given himself away by his manner of walking? Vining had once heard from a Russian diplomat that there were assassins so acute in their senses that they knew by the way a man walked whether he carried a weapon or not. The gun, according to the diplomat, might be a small caliber and weigh mere ounces. It could be nothing more than a pin with a handle, yet these men could tell by the balance of the person that their minds were on the weapon. They were a house of assassins, somewhere in Korea, probably in the north, and so feared by those who knew them that not even the harsh government of North Korea dared trifle with them.

Of course, the Russian diplomat, had said, he did not believe in the tales of their fantastic abilities, but there had been incidents that could not quite be explained, like whole KGB squads being wiped out and when KGB investigators tried to find out how, all they could find were traces and tales of two men, an aged Oriental and a young white.

Who they might work for, the Russians did not know because it was obvious the Central Intelligence Agency did not control them. And if not the Americans and not the Russians and certainly not the Chinese, then who? And if the legend were true, what was a white man doing with those skills when, according to legend, they were passed on only from Korean to Korean, and then, only in that small Korean village that had sent the finest killers out into the world to settle the affairs of Pharaoh and king.

Was he one of them? No, thought Vining. He had probably just seen the gun. Vining believed in nothing that was not for sale, and no one had ever called to offer him the services of these so-called miraculous assassins.

It did not occur to Vining, as he saw Big Jack move his gun hand out from behind his back and push the weapon forward, to ask how the intruder had gotten in unless he could do so-called miraculous things.

"I wanted a pen," came the voice of the intruder in front of Big Jack.

"You'll take this," said Big Jack and the gun went off with a hammering cracking bang. Two times it went, and in the ringing left in the ears of Hastings Vining, he thought he heard the intruder say "Thanks. Thanks a lot."

And there was Jack and he was falling down and there was the gun and it was on the carpet already, with the hand still on it, way ahead of the rest of the body. And there were big black burns in the rug next to the gun. The pistol had been fired by the convulsing nerves of the severed hand, and had singed the rug.

The intruder slipped his right hand under Big Jack as soon as the rest of his body made it down to the rug. The intruder's hand came out with a Bic Banana pen.

"Okay, start from the beginning," said the intruder. "But slow. I don't do shorthand."

"Are you Korean?" asked Vining, not knowing why he dared ask such a question.

"Get off my back," said Remo who was not in a mood to hear about Korea this morning. He was agitated enough about what he was going to do without bringing up Korea and Korean-ness.

Hastings Vining certainly didn't want to be on anyone's back, least of all his honored guest's. Least of all his.

Remo took down the information and at the end had one more little question.

"Yes, anything," said Vining, trying very hard not to look at the right arm of Big Jack because it didn't have any hand on it.

"How do you spell undersecretary? Is that all 'e's or does it have an 'a' in there somewhere?"

"An 'a' in there somewhere," said Vining. "At the end."

"Thanks," said Remo, and finished up by putting Hastings Vining away with a stroke in the frontal lobe up to the knuckles. The eyes were sightless and Vining was dead before he was on the floor.

And Remo realized that moment a deep and abiding truth, told him by a teacher a long time ago in a grade school when old methods of teaching were allowed.

"Remo Williams," she had said so sternly. "You will never learn to spell."

And it was so. He could have sworn there was no 'a' in undersecretary. If he had bet his life on that, he would have bet all 'e's. Going out through the doors was easy. Remo did what he always did in a situation like this. Everyone he saw, and the first were bodyguards, he ordered to get a doctor immediately. No one wanted to be the one who failed to get a doctor when their boss was dying.

And thus, with great leisure, he took the elevator downstairs and when he saw two city policemen running into the hotel lobby, he yelled, "They're still up there and they are armed. Watch out. Here they come."

Which of course meant that the policemen whipped out their revolvers and were looking for cover as was everyone else in this early morning lobby, while Remo walked out onto the street and strolled into the city, looking for an appropriate pay phone. He wanted one inside a store but so few were open. There were restaurants open at this hour, the cheap greasy spoons offering fat-fried starch called potatoes, and dripping pig meat laced with chemicals that attacked the average person slowly, but could do monumental damage to Remo's refined nervous system.

The problem with phoning from one of those restaurants was that grease literally hung in the air and people entering would breathe fat particles into their lungs. While this would not harm the average person and would do just a little damage to Remo, he could taste those places for a week after being in one. And the clothes, of course, would have to be thrown away. When cleaners did manage to get out the grease, they permeated the clothes with disinfectant agents that might peel off Remo's outer layer of skin, unless he concentrated continuously on overcoming it.

It struck him as ironic that in learning and becoming part of the awesomeness of Sinanju and the accumulated knowledge of its centuries of assassins, he had also been made weak in some ways.

Chiun, his teacher, had said it was the great balance of the universe. One received and one gave. One gives pain and weariness and receives strength and stamina in return. Nothing in the world is given that is not taken also and nothing is taken that is not given. Thus had said Chiun, Master of Sinanju. Of course, Chiun had also added that he had given Remo wisdom, discipline, and the powers of the universe and in return had gotten disrespect, sloth, and a general uncaring for a sweet tender soul, gracious beyond belief, that soul being Chiun.

Remo took a partial breath and made it into a Spanish luncheonette open early for workers. There was a payphone in the rear and no one within earshot so he made the call. This was a new number and he had it written down so he wouldn't forget it, and when some small voice inside his head told him he had done this so that upstairs's memory of his last assignment would be of one that was done cleanly and professionally and with no problems, he denied it to himself and said he didn't give a rat's ass what upstairs thought.

Upstairs was Dr. Harold W. Smith, who had, when Remo began his training with Chiun as the sole enforcement arm of the organization, filled Remo with a vision of this one organization, unknown to any but the President, Smith, and Remo himself. And the vision was America's secret weapon to make the Constitution work. To keep government officials honest. To keep the police policing and the prosecutors prosecuting despite corruption in the nation.

It was a great vision. Unfortunately, for whatever little was accomplished, more kept coming apart. CURE just didn't work.

Remo had bought the dream and given his newly learned skills to that dream, and one day he decided that the body and mind could be unified through the basic rhythms of the universe and one did not change people with laws. Instead, people got the law they deserved. If America went down the drain, it belonged there.

It made Remo sad but that was that and he had different obligations now. To his breathing, for one. He understood that, but he didn't understand the Constitution or upstairs or the phone receiver that he could feel vibrate now as he dialed his number.

There was some new kind of scrambler working and as he read from his notes, he realized his voice waves were being sucked into the receiver because it felt as if he was talking with earplugs on. He could only feel his voice inside his mouth. And it sounded different. When he moved his head away from the mouthpiece, he felt the earplug disappear. When close to the receiver, his voice was being sucked into it. Wonderful, he thought. Another piece of worthless junk, designed to make Japanese rich and Americans uncomfortable.

He finished off his report with a request.

"Smitty, can I get a reponse from you or do I have to talk to this computer?"

"You must wait for a response on whether you will get a response," said the computer.

37

Remo made a raspberry into the phone. He noticed an iron skillet filled with yellow potatoes. His breath was unmoving in his lungs. His body rhythms were quiet. His heart kept a very low beat into the blood system. He was not breathing, but he could feel the grease in the air touch his skin. He wanted to scrape it off.

"Okay," came the familiar lemony voice. "Go ahead."

"Smitty, is there an 'a' in undersecretary?"

"Remo, why are you bothering me with that? There are untold problems involving ..."

"Does it have an 'a' or doesn't it?"

"It does, now look, Remo, there's been some unusual activity concerning what might be a growing army and ..."

"It does have an 'a', right?"

"Yes. Now ..."

"Goodbye," said Remo. "Last mission." He hung up and got out into the street where there was breathable air, and inhaled for the first time since before entering the little restaurant. Farther away from the beach, he selected a parked car, slipped in, casually jumped the wires, and drove to Delray down the coast where he parked it several blocks from a marina and walked onto a white two-deck fishing boat, which had been moored there for a month.

He was through. After more than a decade, he had done it. He was through with CURE.

The air was good again and the sea bobbed pleasantly for a man who saw his whole future ahead of him. And he knew what he was going to do with it.

Inside the boat, Remo saw sitting in a lotus

38

position a thin wisp of a man with a wisp of a beard, a wisp of hair over his temples, wrapped in a light blue morning kimono, looking quietly into forever. He did not turn around.

"Little Father," Remo said. "I've quit Smith."

"It is a good morning," said the aged Oriental, and his long fingernails flicked from the robes. "At last. Smith was an insane emperor and there is nothing more dangerous or unbecoming to a great assassin than an insane emperor. Yet, lo, these many years I have not been heard as I warned of this. And why?"

"I don't want to know," said Remo who knew he was going to know whether he liked it or not, and also knew that not even an army could stop Chiun, Master of Sinanju, when he had a point to make. Especially one about Remo's ingratitude and unKorean-ness, or Smith's cheapness and insanity.

Chiun could not understand an organization that wanted to protect a Constitution, and the accumulated history of hundreds of Masters of Sinanju, working for ambitious princes, made it impossible for Chiun to understand the head of an organization who did not want to be emperor. He was shocked early on when Smith refused his offers to assassinate the current President and make Smith emperor in his place. It was this misunderstanding that enabled CURE to hire Chiun's services without his being a danger to the secrecy of CURE.

For, just as Smith would never know Sinanju, Chiun apparently could not know CURE. Only Remo understood most of both, like a man caught between universes, living in one, knowing another, and never finding a home.

39

"Why have I not been listened to, you may ask," said Chiun. He turned slowly, his legs still pointing forward, but his torso spinning completely around toward Remo.

"I'm not asking," said Remo.

"I must answer. Because I have given grace and wisdom and kindness at so little cost."

"Smitty sends an American submarine every year with gold tribute. It risks World War Three by sneaking into North Korean waters to deliver gold to your village. More than Sinanju has ever had from anyone else," said the American part of Remo.

"Not more than Cyrus the Great," said Chiun, referring to the ancient Persian emperor who had given an entire country for services rendered. Ever since, the House of Sinanju had felt highly about working for Persians, even after Persia became Iran. That Iran had billions of dollars of oil did not make it any less attractive to Chiun.

"Too big a gift can be no gift at all," said the Sinanju part of Remo. For Cyrus had given a whole country but, taking command, the Master of Sinanju had learned governing but had lost some of his awesome physical skills. According to the history of Sinanju, he was almost killed before he could pass on to his successor the secrets that came, in diluted form, to be known as martial arts in the west.

Skill lasted forever and was the only true wealth. Nations and gold disappeared but skill passed on would be eternal. This Remo knew. Chiun had taught him as Chiun himself had been taught.

"True," said Chiun, "but it was not the size but the nature of the gift. The gift I have given you is priceless and you have squandered it on an insane emperor. Yet have I ever complained?"

"Always," said Remo.

"Never," said Chiun. "Yet I have borne ingratitude. I have forsaken my own kind, the heirs of Sinanju, for a white. Why have I done this?"

"Because the only one in your whole village who was capable of learning was a traitor to Sinanju and everybody else was no good and when you found me, you found someone who could be a Master of Sinanju, who could pass it on."

"I found a meat-eating pale piece of a pig's ear."

"You found someone who could accept Sinanju, a white man who could learn where a yellow man couldn't. White. White," said Remo.

"Racism," said Chiun angrily. "Blatant racism. And racism is most obnoxious from an inferior race."

"You needed a white man, Chiun," said Remo. "Needed."

"I have cast pearls before a swine," said Chiun. "And swine now claims I needed to throw the pearls away. I have disgraced my House. Lo, there is nothing worse that I can do, nothing worse that can happen."

"I've found another way to make a living, Little Father," said Remo.

And for the first time, Remo saw, on the yellow parchment of the face that had always

41

maintained control as normally as most lungs breathed, a reddish shock fill the cheeks.

And Remo knew he had done wrong. Really wrong.

CHAPTER THREE

Colonel Wendell Bleech got his orders at 4:35 A.M. from the chief himself. They came in the form of a question.

Could he, at this time, pull off one of the initial missions? It was important, because within a short period, the chief wanted to show a fully trained product.

"Can do, sir," said Bleech. He hoisted his pumpkin body up in the bed and made a note of the time the call came in.

"Colonel, it is imperative that you not fail. If you are not ready yet, I'd rather wait."

"We are ready now, sir. Ahead of time." There was a long pause. Bleech waited with the pencil poised over the pad. He heard the even step of his personal guard outside his barracks door. His room was bare as a cell, with only a hard bed, one window, and a trunk for his clothes. Other than the toaster and the refrigerator to keep his English muffins at forty-three-degree temperature and the white enameled bread box holding twenty-two different kinds of jam, the room was without amenities. It was more stark even than his troopers' quarters.

If Bleech needed justification for his harsh discipline, and in his own mind he did not, this room would have sufficed. But he had all the justification he needed in his mission itself. Every time he looked at the two lone pictures in his room beneath the stars and bars of the Confederacy, the old South defeated in the first Civil War, he knew he would do anything for his mission. It was not just another set of orders to him; it was a life's calling. It had led him from the regular army to this special unit, from which there was no recall.

"Colonel, it would be bad if we could not move now, but it would be even worse if we moved and failed."

"We will not fail."

"Can you move tomorrow?"

"Yes," said Bleech.

"Against a city that can be closed off from every exit?"

"Norfolk, Virginia?" guessed Bleech.

"Yes. With the naval base there and lots and lots of hidden protection."

"We can do it."

"Enthusiasm has its limits, Colonel."

"Sir, my enthusiasm ends where my reality begins. I would take this unit anywhere. They're mine and they're good and they aren't messed up with a lot of mollycoddling regular army regulations. This is a fighting unit, sir."

"Go," said the chief in the deep soft voice that the very rich often have because they never have to raise their voices to get anything.

"When do we get the list of . . . er, subjects?" asked Bleech.

"You have it in your Norfolk files. We would like fifteen out of twenty."

"Yes sir. You'll have them within two days."

"I don't want welts on them. No scars either. Welts and scars offend people."

"Not a mark," Bleech promised. "Prime, sir."

Colonel Bleech did not go back to bed but dressed in combat fatigues. He would return to bed in two days. He couldn't sleep now anyhow.

He walked across the main camp compound under the dark misty sky of predawn morning. He smelled the moist heavy breezes of the nearby swamp and heard his solitary footsteps on the parade ground gravel, like crunching drums from an approaching one-man army.

He headed for the intelligence security branch that was leakproof because it was unique. There was no piece of paper in it that could be stolen, that could be given to the FBI or CIA or Congress or anyone who could expose the special unit and what Colonel Bleech now considered his sacred mission.

He had always hated paperwork anyhow. And now he would examine maps and reports and lists without ever touching one piece of paper.

At the north side of the compound, two guards with submachine guns stood over a flat level square of khaki-painted steel.

He nodded to the flat metal square beneath their feet, and thought that if one planted flowers in a cold frame above that door, it could become completely invisible.

The two guards had asbestos gloves clipped to their belts in case Colonel Bleech wanted to enter during the day. The metal shield got awfully hot under the summer sun of South Carolina.

It was comparatively cool now and the two men bent over and put their bare hands under the metal slab. With a grunting effort, they hoisted it, revealing a white concrete stairwell.

Bleech's riding boots made sharp clicking sounds as he descended.

"All right, put it back now," he said, impatiently holding a key at a lock. It would not enter the lock slot unless the heavy metal slab above was shut. The meager moonlight disappeared and the stairwell became dark as a grave as Colonel Bleech pressed his key into the lock, and the door opened and a soft light, increasing gradually, filled the room ahead.

In the center of the room was a console with a screen, one chair, and a set of buttons. This room was simply access to the accumulated intelligence of the cause. When he had seen the room for the first time, when he was initiated into the cause, when the chief himself showed him this room, he knew it was possible to achieve the grand mission.

For here was America at the push of a button, and he pushed Norfolk, Virginia, and he saw the map of the city connected by tunnel and bridge to mainland sections and what security was on each and what the city police did and the state police did and who, as of two days ago, was generally doing what to make the city operate.

He pressed keys for an update and new data flashed onto the console screen. He pressed keys to get the names, locations, and pictures of the twenty. He asked for an update on their whereabouts, no later than noon. He pressed in emergency. The beauty of a system like this, he thought, was that people at the other end of the computer did not have to have any knowledge of who or what they were gathering information for.

Thousands could be working for the cause, and not one would have to know it. Which was why Colonel Bleech believed that it would be possible to achieve the grand mission.

Here he was, looking at the innards of a city, and he was going to go in and neatly take what he wanted, then leave. There was no law or force that could stop him.

Bleech worked out three plans for the raid. It was not like he was inventing them at the moment. He had worked on them for months. He ran them through the computer for an evaluation. And it wasn't that one or at best two would work. They would all work; it was a question of which would work best.

He liked the answers the computer gave back. The assignment was easy, a piece of cake.

The only real problem was the twenty targets. By their nature, they had no exact pattern. Sometimes this pool hall or that bar when the welfare checks arrived, sometimes just an abandoned building. Some would probably be in the hands of the police.

Colonel Bleech refined his plans from the isolated intelligence room as he gave orders to the computer. He was thirsty and hungry and tired and his stomach groaned when he signaled the guards upstairs to open the heavy metal lid.

When they did a light went on in the computer
47

room and a screen against the wall showed who was standing up there. Satisfied that it was the two guards who should be there, Bleech put his key back into the door and walked out. He checked his watch. He and his unit would reach Norfolk with hours to spare. His plan was to keep everyone out until the last possible moment, then make tight sweeps.

He would raid in daylight, for 9 A.M. was the optimum hour, the time when the targets would most likely be asleep in their homes.

When Bleech saw his selected units drive up in drab olive buses, his heart soared. He had planned this but seeing it made him know it would work.

They looked so real in white hats and blue uniforms with white leggings and the SP bands on their arms. They looked like two busloads of Shore Patrol, quite common in a Navy base town. Only Colonel Bleech wore the khaki.

He kept his men waiting in the hot summer sun while he went to sleeping quarters, changed, had four English muffins, and they were off.

They were at the outskirts of Norfolk by dawn and his stomach was hopping with the tension of his first mission. He ordered the two buses into the outskirts of neighboring Virginia Beach, just so they could keep moving without entering the crucial target zones.

He went through an equipment check again. Proper rounds of ammunition per man, proper weapons, the new nylon limb chains—which were far superior to the old heavy metal ones—hypodermic needles, intense sedatives. They were all there.

The buses moved through Oceana, Ocean-bridge, and then, at 8:37 A.M., were in Norfolk and then Granby Street. They drove to the designated check points and then, at this bright morning hour when those who were going to work were at or near work, his unit struck.

The first spot was the Afro-Natural Wig Factory on Jefferson Street, R. Gonzalez, Proprietor. The crew was quickly through the plate glass, ramming it down with two sharp jabs of poles. A beautiful mulatto woman with cream brown skin but fiery black eyes stood inside the entrance of the small shop with a broom. She was brushed aside quickly.

Four men were into the upstairs and the first bedroom on the right. They were down instantly with a groggy drunken young black man.

"This is him. Positive indent, sir. Lucius Jackson."

"That his sister you pushed?" asked Bleech. He looked around. "Where'd she go?"

"That was her."

"Okay, let's go."

The unit was working the street, some groups entering through doors, others through windows. Colonel Bleech knew he could not keep track of the targets because he was too busy making sure officers and men moved as part of one great invasion of this street.

In ninety seconds they were gone, to another street for another raid. Eight seconds later, R. Gonzalez, Proprietor, appeared in the front door of the Afro-Natural Wig Factory, a .44 Magnum in her hand, and cursed when she saw the street was empty. She had wanted to shoot herself somebody.

Bleech was ecstatic. Not a single member of the unit had made a mistake. The intense sedatives worked perfectly. Practiced hands inserted the plastic tongue holders that prevented a drugged person from choking on his own tongue. The nylon chains bound wrists behind backs and feet up tight together at the chest. Like curled laundry bundles, the targets were slid into luggage compartments in the sides of the buses. Unlike the normal Greyhound or Trailways buses, these compartments had oxygen pumped into them.

In four key blocks of this area, they had fourteen men and they had used twenty-two minutes. Bleech made a decision. He could keep looking for the fifteenth target they wanted and expose his group to danger, or leave now with fourteen safely in hand. He decided to leave. It was the right move. He had not been made commander of this special unit because he did not think for himself. He called in all his men.

Trooper Drake, of course, was last. He had a purpose for Drake.

The two Navy buses with their human cargo hidden in the special luggage compartments drove slowly and carefully back to the main street. Every trooper was aboard.

Colonel Bleech gave the order. "Chesapeake Bay Bridge Tunnel," he said to the trooper driving his bus and this order was radioed to the following bus.

So they drove into the tunnel. But the buses that emerged were not Navy buses. They were commercial buses with commercial signs and commercial plates. The panels that had blocked out the windows had been removed and visible inside now were a bunch of college students heading home to Maryland. The troopers had made the switch of clothes and hidden their weapons in eighteen seconds. And it had all been done in a tunnel where no one observed.

Up Route 13 they drove until they reached the outskirts of Exmore. There everyone abandoned the buses carrying bundles labeled Swarthmore State College. Inside these bundles were the shore-patrol uniforms and weapons.

Bleech himself wore a pair of green Bermuda shorts, a white T-shirt reading "Swarthmore State," and a whistle around his neck. He was the coach if they were stopped.

The cargo was left in the luggage compartments, the oxygen machine keeping the bound men alive.

A mile up the dirt road, in a vast meadow, Bleech ordered everyone into the fields to sit and wait.

If Bleech didn't have a wristwatch, he would have sworn that they had waited for a full half hour. But it was only ten minutes. The second hand moved so slowly, and he fully realized in the blazing summer sun how long a minute could be. Then, from over a hill with grass parched brown, came the rackety sound of helicopters. They were on time. They were blue and white and they were beautiful.

And they were on time. He had done it.

There was a message for him when the first chopper landed.

"Sir, fourteen triple perfect," said a pilot who did not know what the message meant. But Bleech knew.

Fourteen meant the number of captives picked up from the buses. Triple perfect meant all three phases of the operation had gone without hitch: Bleech had gotten in and out of Norfolk without any trouble; the fourteen prisoners were exactly what was wanted; and everyone else was doing their job correctly, which meant that the prisoners were already moving toward their final destination.

Bleech loaded his men into the helicopters. Trooper Drake was the last to board and he stumbled getting in.

Back at the base camp, Drake would be accused of not staying with his unit and he would be put into the hot box, a prison that got intensely hot in the summer sun, and then Bleech would march the men for a three-day drill into the woods. Drake would be dead on return and Bleech would make a little speech about how Drake had tried to leave his unit and when a man did that, Bleech just forgot he ever existed. His only problem was whether or not it would be more effective to let the troopers discover Drake dead in the hot box or call them together for a parade, and then open the box calling Drake to walk out. It always carried more terror when your men thought you killed them carelessly, without reason. It gave every potential punishment the spicy threat of fatality.

It was a good unit, Bleech realized. He was running out of men for punishment examples.

52

And now his stomach craved the rich brown points of a toasted English muffin.

He had won his first battle. According to the calculations of the computer and, more importantly, according to his own, the first battle was going to be the toughest. From here on in, it would be easy.

He had done his job and now those who worked the cargo would have to do theirs. But that should be done easily, too. It had been done before. It was only recently, perhaps within the last hundred years, that it had stopped being done in most civilized places.

Lt. Colonel Wendell Bleech did not have the only computer hookup with extremely limited access. There was another, even more extensive in its probes and knowledge of American life, and the access was even more limited. Only one terminal in one spot in America could call out the information, and should anyone else burrow into the computer, the entire unit would self-destruct chemically, becoming a clogged mass of wires and transistors floating in powerful acid.

This computer terminal was in an office in Rye, New York, of what appeared to the outside world as Folcroft Sanitarium. Minimally, it was a sanitarium, but its real purpose was to house the computer complex that was the heart of the secret organization CURE, which now no longer had an enforcement arm.

And what Bleech's computer had told him to do was now being analyzed by the CURE computer and by Dr. Harold W. Smith, the head of the agency, sitting in the office overlooking Long Is-

land Sound and the ocean over which his ancestors had sailed from England to found a country
intended to be based on law.

The early reports were confusing. Either
several men had been snatched or had joined a
raid on a black section of Norfolk, Virginia. The
full facts were not clear this morning because
these were the first reports. Good intelligence,
like good trees, took time to grow and each bit of
information was the fertilizer that helped. So all
Dr. Smith knew at 10:42 A.M. was that some men
were missing. The computer said the men had
certain commonalities, a phrase the brain used
when it was looking for a reason for something.

Smith stared at the commonalities, his lemony
grim face with the thin, tight lips unmoving, but
the mind behind that forehead thinking, yet not
panicking, realizing something was moving at the
nation's innards, and there was still no idea as to
why.

The commonalities of the missing men: they
were all black, between twenty and twenty-three,
and all had petty criminal records. All were
unemployed and unemployable by federal stan-
dards.

Smith took a pencil from his gray vest. He
liked tight vests and gray suits, white shirts, and
his green striped Dartmouth tie. He always wore
cordovans because they lasted longest in his opin-
ion.

He started scribbling. The computers could do
most things better than humans, except to really
roll things around.

The terminal now reported that the number of
missing men was a positive fourteen. Looking

again at the list of common factors among the fourteen men, Smith realized that the people whose lives were affected most by the fourteen men were their relatives, and so he punched into his terminal a request for an early readout on the relatives.

Perhaps one of them had arranged the removal of these fourteen men. Even as he asked the question, Smith knew it was probably wrong. Those who had the most to gain by the disappearance of those missing from Norfolk would be the least likely and least capable of arranging those disappearances.

Only one relative's name came onto the computer, not because it was likely to have arranged the disappearance of the fourteen, but because of a contact with CURE at a previous point. The name was Gonzalez, R., but it was quickly preempted by more important information from the computer: Several witnesses saw subjects being grappled with, bound, and injected with some sort of tranquilizing subject. Those doing it wore Navy shore-patrol uniforms.

Smith asked the computer for a whereabouts on Remo and Chiun. This was done by simply doing what a computer did best, looking through piles of information for something significant. The computer scanned its records, looking for reports of people doing what most people couldn't do. If there were reports from police or newspapers of a single man with bare hands effortlessly crippling many men with guns, that would be an indication. If there was a tale of somebody walking up the side of a building, that would be another. If there was a report of a white and an

55

Oriental involved in a disturbance, caused when someone accidentally touched the Oriental and was dismembered for it, that would have been a conclusive.

This time, the computer gave Dr. Smith only one report. A man had jumped from an airplane without a parachute and lived.

Smith's eyes widened in anticipation and then became their normal steel gray again. The man had indeed jumped from an airplane and lived. He had been injured and was now at Winstead Memorial Hospital, outside of Ramage, South Dakota. His condition was critical.

So much for the whereabouts of Remo and Chiun. They were not at Ramage, South Dakota. It would have taken more than an airplane jump to put Remo in the hospital.

CHAPTER FOUR

The Master of Sinanju had heard it and did not believe it. He would have asked again if he thought he could bear the answer. He asked again.

"What have I done to you that you would commit so foul a deed on me?"

"Maybe it's not foul, Little Father," said Remo.

"I cannot believe it," said Chiun.

"Believe it," Remo said. "I will not kill again."

"Eeeeeeah," said Chiun and Remo's words withered his tired old ears. "The pain I can bear. But knowing that I have betrayed my ancestors by giving so much that will not come back to the House of Sinanju, this I cannot live with."

"I'm not going to feel guilty," Remo said. "I have my life to live, too, and I wasn't born an assassin."

"That need not be mentioned now," said Chiun. And then, in the darkness of his morning, a shaft of light appeared. "You *have* killed, Remo. By your act, you kill. You kill the House of Sinanju by what you do. Who will pass on what we know? Who will take the sun source of the martial arts and give its essence to another to keep it alive? Who, then, if not you?"

"You," said Remo. "You found me. Find some-one else."

"There is no one else."

"What about all those wonderful Koreans you always claim could master Sinanju, but in a moment of weakness you chose a white instead of a Korean? Get one of them."

"I am too old now."

"You're not more than eighty-five."

"I have given so much, there's nothing left."

Remo watched the steaming pot on the boat's butane cooking stove. He was leaving for his new job after this lunch. The rice was steamed perfectly and the duck was a few moments from completion.

He had reservations for a Delta flight out of West Palm Beach to New York City. What he did not mention was that he had reservations for two.

"Do you want ginseng on your rice or not?"

"Ginseng is for happy times. Ginseng is for hearts that have not been broken or betrayed," said Chiun.

"No ginseng?"

"A little," said Chiun. "To remind me of happy days which will be no more." He made sure with his eyes that he got the proper amount. Remo crumbled the root into the boiling pot.

He saw Chiun's face raise a bit, concentrating on the ginseng. He added another pinch. The face lowered.

"But I will not enjoy it," he added. During the meal, Chiun added how he was not enjoying any-thing. Yet he knew there were worse things in the world, he said. Much worse.

"Yeah, what?" asked Remo, chewing his rice to liquidity. Eating, properly pursued, was no more enjoyable at this stage of his development than a breathing exercise. It was, properly done, the taking-in of nourishment. To enjoy it was to do it wrong. For that could lead to eating things for enjoyment instead of nourishment, and that could be fatal, especially to Americans who ate like that all the time.

"You think more of your rice than what I think is a desecration," said Chiun.

"That's right," said Remo.

"Perfidy," Chiun said. "Eternal perfidy. I have one wish in life. And that is never for my eyes to settle upon the waste of Sinanju doing what it was not trained for."

"Okay," said Remo.

"I do not even want to know what you will do."

"Good," said Remo. "It will be better for you that way."

"You know," Chiun said, "not everyone appreciates assassins, no matter how great they are."

"I know," Remo said and there was no mocking in his voice now.

"They call us murderers and killers."

"Well, they have a point. To a degree."

"They don't understand what we do."

"How could they?" Remo asked. He wondered if he needed duck. A young man normally had enough fat in a grain food not to need the duck. A bead of fat glistened on the whitish flesh of the boiled duckling. Remo decided no.

"And in this country, your country, it is worse. You have amateur assassins working everywhere.

Anyone who owns a gun thinks he has a right to kill."

"I know," Remo said.

"But a good assassin, why, even the victims respect him. Because the victim has a better death than if old age attacked, for in old age one is tortured into the grave. One sees one's limbs stiffen and breathing go and eyesight wither and all manner of ills befall. But, when a person goes with the assistance of a great assassin, he lives one moment and all but painlessly does not the next. I would rather be assassinated than be in one of your car accidents," said Chiun.

"I'm going, Little Father," Remo said. "Are you coming?"

"No," said Chiun. "This is too much to bear. Goodbye. I am old and poor. Perhaps you are right and this is the time to leave me."

"You're not poor. You've got gold stashed all over in little packets. And besides, there never has been a time when an assassin can't find work."

Remo packed everything he owned in a small blue canvas bag. An extra pair of chinos, three pairs of socks, four black T-shirts, and a toothbrush.

He thought he would be interrupted by Chiun any moment but the interruption did not come. He zipped up the bag. Chiun worked on his duck, taking little pieces with his long fingernails and chewing them as Remo had chewed his rice, into liquid.

"I'm going," said Remo.

"I see," said Chiun. Remo knew Chiun had

giant steamer trunks that had to be labeled for shipments. He had not asked Remo to label them.

"I'm going now," Remo said.

"I see."

Remo shrugged and let go a sigh. He had worked more than a decade as an assassin and he could not, if he wanted to at this moment, fill his bag with valuables. He was going to a new life. He was going to where he would have a home and a wife and a child. Maybe several children.

Chiun had said children were like orchids, best appreciated when someone else had to do the labor of growing them. They had had this discussion before. Many years before. And many times since.

Remo did not know if he was going to that home and family. He did not know if he really wanted it anymore but he did know he wanted to leave. And he did know he did not want to kill again for a long while, if ever. It was not a big new thing that came on him, rather something that had been coming for so long and so slowly it felt like an old friend whom he had suddenly decided to say hello to.

Chiun did not get up.

"I don't think 'thank you' would be enough," said Remo to the man who had given him that new life.

"You never gave enough," said Chiun.

"I gave enough to learn," said Remo.

"Go," Chiun said. "A Master of Sinanju can do many things. He cannot do miracles. You have allowed yourself to turn into corruption and rot. The sun can make some things grow. It makes others spoil."

61

"Goodbye, Little Father. Do I have your blessings?"

And there was silence from the Master of Sinanju, a silence so deep and so cold that Remo felt the shivers through his bones.

"Well, goodbye," said Remo. And he did not cry. He did not disapprove of those who did; it was just not for him.

Walking down the gangplank to the dock, Remo wanted to take one last look at the man who had given him Sinanju, forever making him someone else from that one-time policeman in that eastern city, who was framed by CURE, lured into its service, and then transformed by Chiun.

He wanted to look but he did not. It was over.

He made the dock, and the sunny day seemed more like a rude heat bothering him. One of the wealthy men from Delray, in blue blazer and yachting cap and a boat that he somehow managed to let everyone know was worth a cool million, which he never had time to run, greeted Remo with his greeting for everyone.

"Hot enough for you, fella?" asked the man from the deck of his yacht and Remo leaped over the railing and slapped tears into his eyes.

Then with his one blue canvas bag he went to the marina office and telephoned for a taxicab to take him to the airport. A secretary using the telephone to talk to a friend was intently describing her previous night, when she told someone triumphantly where to get off.

Remo compressed the telephone into her lap.

She looked horrified at the black shards that had, just moments ago, been a communications link to her friend. And now it was in her lap. The man had crushed the phone as if it had been made of compressed dry cereal.

She didn't say anything. The man who was waiting for the taxi didn't say anything. Finally she asked if she could wipe the plastic pieces and metal parts from her lap.

"What?" asked the man.

"Nothing," she said, sitting very quietly and very politely with a lap full of telephone.

She glanced out the window at a small crowd gathering near a yacht, where one of the wealthier customers was holding the side of his face and gesturing wildly. And alongside that came a most peculiar sight. It was like a blue sheet being propelled by a frail wisp of a man with only a hint of a scraggly white beard, floating up around the dock. She didn't know how he could get around the mob that clustered around the customer holding his face, a mob that stretched from one side of the dock to the other.

The frail little Oriental moving the diaphanous blue robes across the dock did not go around. And the secretary, not wanting to take her eyes off the maniac in her office nor let that incredibly big smile dissipate, because she did not want her steel desk shredded on her, forced herself not to blink. Because the old man in the blue robe didn't go around. He went through, in that strange shuffling gait, unbroken as if the mob didn't exist. And there was the commodore of the marina himself, rolling around on the dock, grabbing his groin in great pain.

And then a horrible thought struck the mind of this secretary, this mind already overloaded with terror. The old man, the Oriental, was coming to the office. He was berthed along with the lunatic who shredded telephones, and he might be even worse, because he moved through crowds as if they did not exist.

And he was coming here. To the office.

She tried to smile harder, but when your jaw is stretched like a two-sizes-too-small leotard, there is no harder to give. So she fainted.

When Remo felt the presence of Chiun moving toward him, the deep brooding darkness torturing his soul suddenly blossomed into sunlight.

"Little Father," said Remo, "you're coming with me. It's the happiest day of my life."

"It is the saddest day of mine," said Chiun. "For I cannot allow the desecration you plan of my gifts and the gifts of the masters of thousands of years of Sinanju to go unwitnessed. I must bear the full pain of your evil."

Chiun folded his long fingernails into his flowing robes.

"We can get your steamer trunks later," Remo said.

"Nothing for you to worry about. They are just my dearest treasures," said Chiun. "Why should I be able to rescue even that meager portion of joy for my life? I have brought a white into Sinanju and now I must pay."

"I'll get them now."

"No," said Chiun. "Do not bother your selfish heart."

"I will."

"I see the taxi," said Chiun.

"He'll wait. I'll carry them on my back."

"I will forego them. I would not trouble the selfish. It is against your nature to do something

64

for another, even for one who has done so much for you."

"I want to," Remo said.

"Yes. I know you do. Carry a trunk. By white arithmetic that equals thousands of years of the powers of the universe. I give you one precious gem, you carry a bag. Well, you're not dealing with some bumpkin from a small fishing village in the West Korea Bay. You can't cheat me like that. Come, we go."

"The bags aren't here, are they?" said Remo.

"It doesn't matter that they were shipped days ago to a picking-up point. What matters is that you thought carrying them equaled what I gave you. That's what mattered. That's why I am here. I must see with my own eyes the degradation to which you have put the sun source of all hand fighting. I must suffer this evil because I have created it. And you will never cheat me again by carrying a bag."

And thus did Chiun, having planned all along to go with Remo, escape not only having to admit so, but once again showing how the world ill repaid his awesome kindness and decency.

The business Remo was going into, taking his skills with him, was advertising. Chiun knew of advertising and they discussed this on the Delta flight out of West Palm Beach to New York City.

Chiun knew of advertising. Before soap operas had been degraded by including the unpleasant things of life, Chiun had watched all of them closely and in so doing had become aware of the selling of household products in America. They were, he knew, mostly poisons.

"You will not be handling soaps?" asked Chiun,

horrified at the thought of burning lye and fat on Remo's skin. He had been so pale when Chiun had gotten him for training years before and now with the health back in his skin, Chiun did not want it washed away with American poisons.

"No. I'm going to demonstrate a product."

"You are not going to put white chemicals in your body?"

"No," Remo said.

"Aha," said Chiun and there was joy in his face for he knew. "How could I have misjudged my training? How could I have felt you would desecrate what I have taught you? My gift is beyond desecration."

"Little Father," said Remo hesitantly. "I don't think you understand."

"Of course I understand. Americans may be white but they are not complete fools. They will say look, look at the wonders of Sinanju and you will demonstrate on some boxer or whoever they think is strong the awesomeness of Sinanju. And then they will say Sinanju has its power by eating one of whatever they are selling. And then you will say you have eaten that as part of your training, which also explains the greater mystery of why they have asked you to demonstrate and not me. I have one request. When you say how good the product is and you put it in your mouth, chew, don't swallow, because all American food is poison."

"It's not that, Little Father. I'm not going to demonstrate Sinanju."

"Oh. I feared that," Chiun said and he was quiet until just over New York City when he had a question. "Will you appear on television?"

"Yes."

"Are you not supposed to be modest and secret? You do everything so that people will not recognize our glories. This is part of your inscrutable white character. But your face will surely be recognized."

"They won't be filming my face. They'll be filming my hands."

And Chiun thought about that too but he knew it was foolish because Remo's hands would never be able to show how mild a soap was. They were more sensitive than women's hands. And that was for women's commercials for women's soaps. Men's commercials sold soaps strong enough to be used as tortures.

It was a vicious white cycle. First they ate meat fats that gave them a rancid flavor, then they scrubbed off the putrescence with poisons.

"If not soap, what?" asked Chiun.

"Do you remember the first exercises for the hands?"

"Which one? There are so many."

"The orange," said Remo.

"Peeling," said Chiun.

"Right. The one where I learned that the hand is a function of the spinal cord by peeling an orange with one hand."

"It's hard for children," said Chiun.

"Well, I was doing it at the marina and I met this investor and . . ."

As Remo told the story, it was a typical tale of disaster, starting out with a wonderful idea and lots of money. A growth company with a knack for massive fast profits got a report on home-tool use, showing the kitchen area was "about to maximize a new base growth," which meant that people were going to spend more money on kitchen things.

The report said many expensive gadgets were going to be sold, and if someone could offer a competitive but cheaper gadget, they could make a fortune using television advertising.

So the marketing people told the engineers they wanted a kitchen gadget that could chop and puree, grind and slice, and sell at $7.95. It should also dice carrots. It should cost less than 55 cents to make and less than 22 cents to mail. It should be no larger than two average coffee cups and be made of red plastic and clear plastic with a piece of shiny metal in it, because surveys showed red plastic and clear plastic with shiny metal were looked upon favorably by 77.8 percent of American women.

The engineers did a miraculous job filling every requirement. Marketing said they could sell ten million in a month with an advertising budget that was included in the 55 cents production cost.

Tears had come to the man's eyes as he told Remo that the 55 cents included the advertising budget. At this point in his story, the man had cursed the fates and the unknown mysteries.

Chiun listened to Remo relate this story as they left the airplane. He had never understood white thinking but he had to admit they made good airplanes and television sets and, before viciousness and wanton sexuality had overtaken them, good daytime dramas called soap operas. What was wrong with the American product, wondered Chiun.

"It didn't work," said Remo. "Guy said everything was perfect but it didn't work. Now they've got a couple of million of those doohickies in a warehouse and if they don't start moving them in the next couple of days, they start to lose money. He's got it down to the fraction of a penny."

"I do not see how a simple exercise such as peeling an orange would have anything to do with his product," said Chiun.

"When he saw me peel the orange, he thought I might be able to use the Vega-Choppa."

"Vega-Choppa?" said Chiun, motioning a taxi outside the airport to move on because its insides were not clean enough. The driver said that if Chiun wanted to wait for a clean cab, he would have to move to the end of the line.

The driver was later treated at Queens Memorial Hospital.

Chiun got a clean cab into New York. "I always like these flesh-colored vehicles when they are clean," he confided to Remo. "Now what is a Vega-Choppa?"

"That's the gadget. Computers worked out the name. It's some plastic junk and a strip of metal, seven dollars and ninety-five cents. He figured if I could peel the orange I could do the commercial for it with my hands."

"And did you?"

"That's where we're going now. See, they couldn't sell the thing on television 'cause they couldn't find anybody to demonstrate it. But he had one and it's no big thing. It's timing, if you have your timing, you can cut carrots and tomatoes and everything. It'd be easier to do it with a broken bottle, but I'm not getting paid to do it with a broken bottle."

At the studio, the lights were on and the camera crews were ready. Chiun watched disdainfully. The Vega-Choppa was the size of a woman's hand.

Remo got his instructions on which vegetables to cut first. This would be photographed while the announcer read the cue cards in front of him.

There were ripe tomatoes, a banana, a bunch of carrots, and a head of lettuce on a wooden table. Many lights shone on the table.

A small intense woman put sleeves, without arms, on Remo's thick wrists. The sleeves were the same color as the jacket on the announcer. A table identical to Remo's was wheeled in front of the announcer. Another table with artistically cut vegetables was uncovered to the far right. The announcer was in the center and Remo was at the left.

There were three cameras and not one was focused on Chiun, who made a mental note to add to the history of Sinanju, under the chapters of "Chiun and the Americans," how American taste in entertainment was highly peculiar, as one might expect from beefeaters.

"We're going to do something very dangerous," came a voice from the dark part of the studio. "We're going to shoot all this live, on tape, without the voice being dubbed. That's the kind of faith we have in this product and, of course, you, sir, what's your name?"

"Remo."

"What's your first name?"

"That is my first name."

"Well, we'll just call you 'Hands,' all right? When you see the light, begin."

"Call me Remo, not 'Hands.' "

Two lights on two cameras flashed red. Remo waited.

"You want a food machine?" asked the announcer as Remo picked up the Vega-Choppa and a tomato. "You want to pay one hundred or two hundred dollars or more and then run up electricity bills? Or do you want a magic food machine in your hands?"

Gripping the blade of the Vega-Choppa lightly, Remo threw it toward the hand with the tomato in it. Chiun alone could see through the speed of it that Remo's hands were pressing the tomato around the blade, an intricate maneuver very much like pressing flower petals into bamboo strips, so that the petals were not damaged but the strips were cracked. Remo did this several times, so that the blending of the tomato around the blade looked as if the blade was cutting the tomato into slices.

"Tomatoes are a cinch," said the announcer. "You slice as many as you want and when you're done, perhaps you want cole slaw. You say you can't make cole slaw without shredding? Hours and hours of shredding? Don't pay high prices for slaw in your supermarket. Now, hours of drudgery and high supermarket prices are gone. You have slaw as easily as tomatoes or potatoes or diced carrots or apples that peel magically with your Vega-Choppa."

Remo's hands flew. He got the blade going back and forth by compressing the action through the vegetables, a technique of hand action known to Sinanju since the time of Genghis Khan, when certain tribes used reed shields that were quite effective against metal spears.

If a student were talented, he could master this in eight years of training.

Out of Remo's sight, Chiun nodded approval. The hands were working well. Unfortunately, no one other than Chiun could appreciate the esoteric and incredibly skilled function now being performed and labeled "as easy as apple pie," the apple now being shredded into little slices.

"And what does this miracle tool cost? Not one hundred dollars. Not fifty dollars. Not even twenty-five dollars. It's just seven ninety-five and with it—if you send in your order within six days—you get the miracle carrot peeler."

With only a useless sliver of shiny metal, Remo scraped the skin of a carrot and Chiun had to force himself not to applaud. It was so difficult to manipulate the peeler that Remo could have skinned the carrot more easily with his knuckles.

"And carrots," said the announcer. "As easy as that."

It was a good performance. So easy had Remo made it look that when the cameras were off, the announcer just wanted to slice a tomato to see the even round pieces fall like playing cards.

He was unable to break the skin of the tomato and finally leaned on the Vega-Choppa with both hands, creating a popping mush, and getting a gouge in his thumb and forefinger that needed five stitches to close.

Chiun was proud but sad. Remo had used his skills well, but in a wrong cause, and if the rest of

Remo's life was to be spent demonstrating tools that no one could use, then Chiun would have to think seriously of finding another student to build into a new Master of Sinanju.

CHAPTER FIVE

She saw the hands. She saw them on the TV
screen and she knew it was him. She stopped yelling at workmen repairing the glass in the front
of her wig factory and shop, the finest wig shop
in Norfolk, Virginia—unless of course you
wanted something in a cheaper line, like rayon,
which was not only blonder but could wash better
and wear longer. And when you got tired of looking like a giant yellow mum, it made the best
mattress stuffing this side of down. The Gonzalez
Wig Emporium also sold down, imitation down,
stuffing, life insurance, and Jesus bracelets that
fought gout.

She stopped yelling and she looked.

"Remo," she said.

"What?" said one of the workmen.

"Keep sweepin', nigger," said Ruby Gonzalez
who was just a partial shade lighter than the
brown workman. She knew she wasn't beautiful
but she had an attractive presence that would not
quit; when she set her eyes on a man, she could
make him hers.

And maybe that was what was needed now, because she had just seen the hands of a man who
could do miracles. Who might be able to get Lu-

cius back—Lucius, who had been dragged screaming out of the shop, screaming, until the attackers could get a needle into him. No one knew who had seized the fourteen missing men and still a week later no one knew where they were. Although Ruby had her suspicions. But what good were suspicions when you didn't have the muscle?

And special muscle she needed. Some dummy with a gun would not do. She had seen them. If they got the guy you wanted, they more than likely shot up half a town. Norfolk was a quiet town. She got along in Norfolk. She had friends in Norfolk. Ruby didn't want to shoot up the town to get her brother back. With the help of those hands on television she might be able to.

Remo. She had never been able to find him again.

It was at a time she was working for the government, when because of her black blood and Spanish surname and female gender she had become an entire equal opportunity program in the hands of the CIA. She meant that they didn't have to hire quite as many blacks, women, or Spanish surnames. Which was not all that bright, Ruby knew, because she was the only one in her department who didn't make a botch of things.

For a woman of twenty-three, she was wise in the ways of the world. She was not afraid her country was going to be devastated by some great sinister foreign intelligence agency. She understood very well that most white men were stupid. As were black men. And yellow men. And that included the white man and the yellow man she had met on assignment in Baqia, one of those stupid

75

places nobody wanted until somebody else was about to get it.

She had never been able to find a trace of them again. Remo's fingerprints were not on file anywhere her friends could get to. It was like he and Chiun had vanished, but here she saw those hands on TV, just when she needed them most.

"Mama, Mama," she yelled, running to the small apartment above the shop. Mama liked living here. Ruby lived in a mansion out of town. She had offered her mother several rooms in the Gonzalez mansion in Princess Anne County, but her mother wanted to stay with her old friends in Norfolk. Mama also liked to eat. Mama was not allowed to eat in the mansion. Ruby had it up for resale and she didn't want crumbs on the floor.

"Mama, Mama," cried Ruby. "I think we can save Lucius."

Mama sat in a blue painted rocking chair smoking a pipe. Mama smoked chicory, corn silk, and dried maple leaf ground together. Some said this combination caused neither bronchitis nor cancer nor any other disease, because it acted not so much like a carcinogen as a razor. It would lacerate your throat before it would pollute it.

Most people passed out from sniffing it. Ruby had grown up with it.

"They gonna save Lucius?" asked Mama, her tired face a rich deep black, the wrinkles warm with many a weary year of going on from day to day.

"No. We're gonna save him," Ruby said.

The old woman thought about this a long moment. She took a deep puff on her corncob pipe.

"Chile?" she said.

"Yes, Mama," said Ruby.

"What yo' want to do that for? He de most useless chile in this Lord's creation."

"He's my brother, Mama."

"I'm sorry about that, chile, but sometimes I think maybe dey made a mistake at de hospital, ceppin' I didn' go to no hospital. Maybe we made a mistake on de kitchen table."

"Mama, that's Lucius we're talking about. He may be hurt."

"Only if he working. That boy only hurt when he work. Sometime ah think maybe we get him mixed up with a loaf of bread or something that day on de kitchen table but then ah remembers we only eats white bread. And sometimes ah try to pictorialize zactly in my mind what we throw away in de kitchen that day. Was it de afterbirth or Lucius that got dumped wif de garbage? Ah use to think we kept de afterbirth, but afterbirth don' eat, do it?"

"No, Mama."

"Then that's Lucius. De eatenest baby ah ever see."

"Mama, he's been kidnapped."

"Ah know. His bed be empty from nine in the morning to five at night, Monday until Friday, all this week. Ah know something be wrong."

"I'm going to get him back," Ruby said. "And I know how. There are two men who can do miracles, Mama, and I've just seen their hands on television. I'm going to get him back. Lucius is a good boy."

"Lucius de most useless chile in dis here country. He don't even pick up welfare checks.

77

When de mail was late dat week, he call de mayor, saying dems oppressin' him. Dat boy never did a lick of work in his life. Boy even gave up muggin' 'cause people stopped walkin' down dat alley behind de shop. He say he ain' traveling to work no ways."

An ordinary executive might have been turned off in her search for the owner of the hands. But Ruby Gonzalez, owner of Wig Emporium, Wig City, a wig factory, two real estate agencies, a mail order house, and director of four banks, was not about to be put off by some clerk just because he had the title of vice president for marketing.

"Madam, let me assure you we used only a regular announcer for that commercial, an announcer who has been doing these things for years. We did not import specialized skills for the easy operation of the miracle Vega-Choppa, the bestselling kitchen appliance since the pot. Heh, heh."

"Turkey, I know those hands. Now you going to help me or not help me?"

"We have been one of the leading ad agencies in America since our inception in Philadelphia in 1873. We do not engage in fraud."

Within forty minutes, Ruby had a history of the ad agency showing it had begun with a flyer claiming Dr. Magic's Wonder Grease cured brain tumors, and in 1943 had been indicted for claiming cigarette smoking promoted sexual vitality, clear skin, and long life.

When they met again, the vice president for marketing admitted to Ruby that the hands she saw were represented by a major talent agency that handled actors and writers. The hands had been given to a young agent because no one knew what to do with hands. The agent generally represented marginal writers. By marginal, the agency meant that if one of their agents had to do more than pick up a telephone to get a half million-dollar advance on a book, the writer of the book was marginal.

The hands had been rejected at the actor's section of the agency because both the man and his Oriental friend lacked what Hollywood considered "an essential sense of danger. We don't get a feeling that the hands have a person attached to them who can give the audience that sense of danger we get from leading stars."

And that made Ruby even more sure that the hands were those of Remo and the Oriental was Chiun, who was all right if you stayed on his right side. Remo was all right, too, but he was "real country" as Ruby liked to say. And he was funny, although he thought he was the most serious dude in the world. As for sanity, she would have bet on Chiun. She could understand why Chiun did things; there was no explaining what Remo did. Like making commercials.

She flew up to New York to meet Remo's agent.

The agent was so pretty he made Shirley Temple look like a concrete septic tank. He was so neat his lips looked as if moisture on them would be a mess. It was the first time Ruby ever wanted to be a man. If she were a man, this beautiful young man might be interested in her.

"I want those hands," said Ruby.

"Gawd, who doesn't, dear?" the agent said and Ruby wondered how he kept his hair that right.

Her $9.95 rayon wig didn't come out of the machine that neat. As a matter of fact, nothing was that neat.

"Yeah, but I want to do a commercial on some of my stuff," said Ruby. "I want those hands in the commercial. So call them."

"Well, actually, we don't call them. They call us."

"Tell me where they are. I'll call them," Ruby said.

And because it was all so boring, trying to track down properties who had just hands when there were so many big things going on out there, the agent gave Ruby the address.

The two were in a luxury hotel overlooking Central Park. They had a suite. They were registered as "Jones and the gracious one."

When Ruby stood outside their door, she suddenly became weak for a moment. She remembered the Island of Baqia and the miracles Remo and Chiun did and she remembered how often she had thought of them since that time.

But Ruby Gonzalez was Ruby Gonzalez and when she knocked and heard Remo's voice ask who it was, she answered, "None of your business, dodo. Open this door."

When the door opened, all she could say was, "Hello." And her voice was weak.

"Hello," said Remo. "Where you been?"

"Around," she said.

"Yeah," said Remo. "I've been there, too. What brings you here?"

And Ruby Gonzalez took a deep breath and concentrated and began talking a mile a minute, "Because you two owe me. I save your life and you make me promises and then you just go and get lost and you never deliver on your promises and I shoulda known you never would, not you two, and now I'm here to collect."

"Same Ruby," sighed Remo. "Screeching at me. For a minute there, I thought it was going to be different."

But Chiun had seen the look on Ruby's face. He knew it was different, that different emotions had entered Ruby's heart, and while he said, "Come inside, close the door, and get the rice boiling," he was thinking that maybe he had found the way to get a new trainee for the House of Sinanju. One that nobody else would have a chance to mess up.

"Hello," said Ruby, stepping inside the door.

"Animal," said Chiun. "Animal. Rutting animals. Blacks, whites. Sexually active, mentally dormant. I see the looks in your faces, the both of you. I suppose you two want to make love now."

There was no answer.

"I suppose I should be grateful you two don't fall on the rug and couple there," said Chiun. But when they didn't, Chiun decided he had had it with the subtle approach.

"A thousand gold pieces for a male child from the loins of my son," he called out.

"Five thousand," said Ruby.

"Three thousand," said Chiun.

"Wait," said Remo. "Don't I have anything to say about this?"

"No," said Chiun. "Who listens to a television star?"

"No," said Ruby. "You got nothing to say."

CHAPTER SIX

Lucius Jackson Gonzalez was too busy to wipe the sweat off his brow. He had been on this assembly line since daybreak and was still one hundred units short of his goal. His body twitched with terror.

"Speed up the line," he begged.

From above him on a metal ramp, he heard the overseer's metal-tipped boots clack toward him.

"Quiet," came the gruff voice. Lucius Jackson Gonzalez did not know the face. He did not often look up to see it.

"Yes sir," he said and just prayed that they would speed up the assembly line so he could get his one hundred additional units.

It had only been a week since he had been ripped out of his bed at the strange hour of nine A.M., but that seemed like only a vague memory of a time so sweet and lazy he could hardly remember it. Now, all he remembered was the round metal bands he was supposed to wrap securely around the wooden posts that passed him on the assembly line. Late in the day, the work became more difficult as the wooden posts wore down and you had to take more care with the bands.

In the morning the metal just slipped in and it was secure and nobody was going to say anything. But down the assembly line, where six men used tools to take the bands off, the slots in the wood would wear down. And the bands themselves had to be handled gingerly because if you just snapped them on late in the day, they might break. Metal became tired. And all these problems mounted as the day wore on.

Lucius's right hand suddenly spouted a red leak. He tried to hold back the blood so it wouldn't get on the bands. He had seen them go down the production line with blood on them before and the overseer always found out who did it. Lucius did not want to be found out so, wounded, he worked and prayed.

It was not a slow transformation that had brought him to this eager sweating service. He had been sleeping. And what he remembered was hands grabbing him and he thought it might have been the police, except they would have been afraid to touch him. Police had to read you your rights. Police had to refrain from undue violence. You pretty much had to cut up a policeman before he would put his hands on you.

So when Lucius felt the hands, he knew immediately it wasn't the police. And he tried to reach for his razor, because when you were dealing with a brother, you had better cut first. But he couldn't get to his razor. And then he saw the men were white.

He was working on his lawsuit charging a violation of his civil rights when he felt something very sharp prick his arm and then everything became heavy in his head and very dark.

He thought he was still falling when he realized he couldn't move his hands or legs and there was a plastic thing on his tongue. He thought he was blinded at first because there was only darkness around him. Then he saw a flat plane of very white light coming in down at his feet. And he saw other bodies in the shaft of light. His mouth was dry and he could not close it to swallow. The thirst became a biting pain and then numb. He could not feel the right arm his head rested on. His left was growing numb. He knew they were traveling because he could hear the motor and feel the bumping of the road beneath him.

Then, the engine stopped and suddenly there was blinding light at his feet and he felt himself yanked out into the light that was too bright to see. Rough hands pulled back his eyelids. His eyes burned.

"This one's all right," said someone. The plastic that wrapped his tongue and kept his mouth open was yanked out. Blessed cool water came in and Lucius lapped it up eagerly. He gulped and swallowed until his belly was full. The bindings on his wrists and ankles came off. And numbing pain came to his right arm on which he had rested.

He was too frightened to talk. As he looked around he saw friends he knew, their eyes wide, laying on the ground or kneeling. Piles of white nylon ropes lay in pieces before him. When he could use his eyes, he saw there were two big buses behind him and their luggage compartments were open wide.

He shook his head trying to get the grogginess out of it.

He was standing on a grass lawn. In front of him was a mansion. Behind him, the ocean stretched to the horizon. A small yacht was tied up at a dock at the water's edge.

White men with whips and guns stood several paces away. They wore white suits with white straw hats.

They said nothing.

Lucius saw a friend of his, Big Red, who did pimping whenever he found a girl he could terrorize. Big Red was a bad dude. Even police didn't want to mess with Big Red. Lucius felt better because Big Red was there. Big Red was a Lasufi Muslim and had changed his name to Ibrahim Al Shabazz Malik Muhammid Bin. Lucius Jackson Gonzalez had been planning to change his name, too, but it was too much work, having to go to court and all, so he settled for just unofficially dropping the Gonzalez and being known as Lucius Jackson.

He tried to smile at Big Red. He was happy that he was there. Nobody messed with a Lasufi Muslim. These white tormenters would soon be put in their place.

One of the black men shouted "We gonna have yo' ass for this."

Wordlessly, a tall thin man with a thin smile and red hair, the sort of person you might lean on for a few dollars in a deserted street, came out of a car. He had a sword. He cut off the head of the man who shouted. Lucius watched the head roll. He also saw Ibrahim Al Shabazz Malik Muhammid Bin suddenly lower himself to his knees, then bend forward till his forehead touched the ground. His flat hands were by his ears. A low wailing moan came up from Big Red's mouth. It was a spiritual. Man, did he love Jesus now.

In an instant, the avenging Islamic terror of Norfolk, Virginia, was born again as a Christian.

There was never an argument after that and it seemed Lucius Jackson had been working on the assembly line forever, along with the other twelve survivors. Seven putting on metal bands; six taking them back off. Lucius didn't question the need for such work. He would do whatever he was told. When they heated his twice daily gruel, he was most thankful for the gift. One day, somebody put a piece of pork in the gruel and Lucius, who'd only eaten well-marbled meats before and shouted at Ruby if she bought him T-bone instead of porterhouse, almost cried with joy. On the day they got real bread and real beans, Lucius almost kissed the hand that fed him.

The diet of Lucius Jackson was no accident. It had been carefully planned as the minimum to sustain strength and to create a sense of, first, dependency and, then, gratitude in the recipient.

Eight men, representing some of the most powerful corporations in the world, received this information in a bound booklet they had yet to open. They had been called to West Palm Beach, Florida, by Baisley DePauw, national executive chairman of the National Urban Movement, a group dedicated to alleviating poverty, urban regression, and racism. The DePauws had been involved in liberal American causes ever since they stopped union busting with machinegun-toting goons.

American school children never learned how the family that ordered machine guns to open fire on unarmed strikers at one of their oil refineries could have become so dedicated to the welfare of the citizens in so many public causes. When one thought of the DePauws, one thought of commissions fighting racism. When one thought of the DePauws, one thought of an angry warning to South Africa on its apartheid policies. When one thought of the DePauws, one thought of the angry young playwrights they sponsored who produced such plays as "Good Honkey, Dead Honkey."

The DePauws also sponsored conferences where business leaders heard militant blacks ask for money for guns so they could shoot the business leaders. This suggestion was called an "in-depth rage."

This conference in West Palm Beach, however, was not another progressive venting of the spleen. Baisley DePauw had promised that and had personally phoned each of the eight men. And each conversation went like this:

"This is business, real business. Don't send me some vice president you keep around to attend the meetings you don't think are important. Let me tell you how important this meeting is."

"Please do."

"Anyone who is not at this meeting will not be able to compete in the marketplace within two years."

"What?"

"You heard me."

"C'mon, Baise, that's hard to believe."

"Do you remember that little project I told you about a few years ago?"

"The big secret?"

"Yes. Well, it worked. What if I told you I could man one of your production lines with workers at a cost of less than forty cents a day? Not an hour, a day. And what if I told you you would never have to worry about strikes again? What if I told you you would never have to worry about working conditions or pensions? What if I told you your workers would worry only about getting old and useless?"

"Baise, I'd say you're full of shit."

"Either you come to that meeting or don't send anyone."

"Dammit, I've got a personal meeting with the President of the United States that day."

"Two years, out of business. Take your choice."

"Baise, move the thing back a day."

"No. I'm right on schedule."

Baisley DePauw invited eight men and eight men showed up. The base kernel of western industry sat around a long table in the DePauw mansion in West Palm Beach. There would be no drinks because it required a servant to bring drinks. They would not be allowed to have their secretaries present because eight was the limit who could know this thing. Anyone who didn't have to know it couldn't.

"Baisley, old boy, this is rather much of a precaution."

"It is a daring idea," said Baisley DePauw.

And Baisley DePauw, the very model of concerned patrician elegance, from the touch of gray at his temples to the rolling Hudson River accent, bade his guests to open their bound booklets. Most of them didn't understand what they read. They complained that they had people who understood these sorts of things. They weren't labor relations experts. They made decisions on how most of the civilized world lived. They couldn't be bothered with labor costs. If Baisley wanted to play with trivia, why didn't he have this at a lower level?

"Your labor costs and labor attitude is why Japan gains on us every day. Your labor costs determine how you do business now and in the future. It's getting worse. You're paying more for less."

"And you're no different, Baise. C'mon," said the chairman of a conglomerate that had just given a contract whereby men would retire with more than they used to make ten years earlier. When someone mentioned labor costs to him, all he could think of was high. He also got very sick when someone mentioned these things. And not being in front of labor people, he could afford to spit when DePauw mentioned labor costs. So he did. On the rug.

"We also have problems with the inner cities," said DePauw. "You know the costs of the urban poor. How they act on an environment. I'm talking about the native American black, the original American slave. If you compress what they do to an area, like say the South Bronx in New York City, it's like a bombing raid during World War Two. Except more expensive."

Now when DePauw began mentioning inner city and blacks, the executives became restless. If they were not all that interested in labor statistics, they cared even less for social causes, although every one of them had appeared in pictures receiving plaques for their work in civil rights. They had all joined fashionable organizations contributing millions to black causes. They had condemned racism. They had even joined appeals to end racism and testified in Congress against racism. Thus was American industry against racism, because as one of them put it, "The cost is negligible and we really don't have anything to do with those people." Another called it "cheap virtue."

Baisley DePauw picked up a picture of a black man.

"Dammit," one industrialist yelled. "If you want to discuss social programs, do it somewhere else. You're wasting our time with this crap."

"I am showing you a resource," said DePauw. He had dealt with these men and taken their measure, and their anger was just where he wanted it.

He showed a photograph of Lucius Jackson. "Resource," he said.

Someone guffawed. "That is about as much a resource as cancer," said a computer executive.

Baisley DePauw allowed a thin knowing smile to cross his face.

"This man, part-time pimp, part-time mugger, on and off welfare I don't know how many times, father of countless children he doesn't support, is now a fine worker who costs the manufacturer forty cents a day and, if he does reproduce, will give us another fine worker just like himself. Better workers than you have. And no union leaders to fight with."

"I don't believe it. I don't believe in social programs."

"That's why I brought you down here. Gentlemen, just a few feet from here is my proof. We are going to revolutionize American labor practices, undercut Taiwan and Hong Kong on prices, and make our cities once again the playthings of the rich."

DePauw took them down to a subbasement and what the eight executives saw shocked them. There was a white man with a whip at one end of the small room. Thirteen black men stood at a conveyor belt. The first seven busily wrapped a metal band around a wooden pole and the last six busily unwrapped it. The men worked at a steady pace that did not slacken. They had chains on their ankles.

DePauw stood on a small balcony overlooking the work room. He yelled out to the first man in the line, "If you could have anything, what would you want?"

And Lucius Jackson smiled and said, "Sir, the only thing ah wants is for the line to be speeded up so I can meet my quota, sir."

DePauw turned and nodded, then closed the door behind him and took the eight executives back upstairs to his office suite.

One said, "We are talking about slavery. We are talking about the enslavement of human beings for profit. We are talking about the most reprehensible use of one human by another."

DePauw nodded. The other executives crowded around.

"We are probably talking about another civil war," said the executive.

DePauw nodded again.

"We are talking about violating every civilized principle known to mankind."

"Not every one," said DePauw. "We will not desecrate private property."

DePauw watched these powerful men exchange glances. He knew the question that was coming. He knew as surely as he had known many of these men since childhood. He knew he was proposing a revolution with more real change in how people lived than any that had been done in Russia.

"Baise," said the executive who had been doing the major share of questioning. "You know you have raised a very, very serious question here."

"I know," said DePauw.

"Can you," said the executive and now everyone hung on every word and everyone watched DePauw for his answer.

"Yes?" said DePauw, waiting for what he knew would come.

"Can you . . . get skilled workers?"

"You bet your ass," said DePauw. "Skilled workers. The cheapest work force since the Confederacy. Gentlemen, we will break the unions with the best scabs who ever lived. Slaves."

But some had doubts. It sounded too good to be true. DePauw pointed out that blue collar workers, who would ultimately lose the most from a slave labor force, would be the biggest supporters.

"I have a military arm already in operation," said DePauw, "but I don't think we'll ever need it. What I think we're going to do is to create a public sentiment so overwhelming that millions of people are going to fall in step behind our army and march on Washington and make them do what we want. We'll have a referendum and we'll carry it ten to one."

"You think Americans would vote to create a labor force that would wreck their own bargaining power?"

"I've been working on this plan since the sixties. Why do you think I financed all those militant blacks on television shows? You know who watched them? An eighty-one percent white audience. And when they were through, the whites who watched showed an overwhelming desire to shoot blacks. We have the old films of blacks saying they were going to get whitey. We've financed more black television this year than ever before. Next week we start our real advertising program, and just as it gets underway, nobody in America will be able to turn on a television set without seeing a black face telling them how if they don't move on over, he's going to move on over them. It's beautiful."

"Too bad Malcolm X is dead," said one executive. "You could have given him a TV series."

"We've got something just as good. A sociology professor telling whites how rotten they are and then in the background we show films of Harlem and the South Bronx and Watts and Detroit."

"But you'll never be able to get a national referendum on slavery."

"Oh, come on," said DePauw, a bit annoyed. "We're not going to call it that. It will be an affirmative action law, giving blacks a right to security and whites the right to safe streets. I haven't gotten this far thinking the American people know what they're doing. My family came over to this country in seventeen eighty-nine and we haven't stopped stealing since, and the only time we take a break is to receive a good citizenship award."

There was silence in DePauw's office suite.

"Baise, I don't know if the public will vote for it," said one executive.

"They've got to," said DePauw.

"Why?"

"I've got a real big advertising budget," DePauw said.

CHAPTER SEVEN

There were police reports, newspaper reports, and in-depth analyses of the strange disappearance of the more than a dozen urban poor. Newspapers were still unsure of how many had really disappeared at the time of the invasion incident in Norfolk, because some might just have moved on to another town.

Chiun heard Ruby explain everything. She said her sources were better than newspapers or police.

"And what are you telling us all about it for?" asked Remo.

"Because I checked and the CIA don't know anything and I figured that organization of yours probably knows and you and the old gentleman can help me get Lucius back."

"First of all," Remo said, "I'm not working for that organization anymore. I quit. Second, why should I help you get Lucius back?"

"Because I saved your life and you owe me."

"And I got you out of jail," Remo said, "back on Baqia. So we're even."

"Not even," said Ruby. "Not even. I was gonna be getting out of that jail anyway and you just messed it up."

"Well, I won't mess this up. Find Lucius your-self," Remo said.

"I saved your life," Ruby said. "I saved your life."

Chiun, seeing the possibility of Ruby and Remo presenting him with a male offspring slowly vanishing, nodded his head. "Remo, this is a debt unpaid. She gave us our lives, we must give her the life of this Lucius, whoever he is."

"My brother," said Ruby.

"See, Remo?" said Chiun. "Such devotion to family. Such a woman is a fine woman. She would make a wonderful mother for a male child."

"Knock it off, Chiun," said Remo. "I'm not going into stud service for Sinanju. All right, Ruby, we'll help you get your brother back. But we're not going to do it with the organization. I've quit and that's that."

"All right," said Ruby.

They went back to Norfolk, Virginia, and Chiun insisted that he and Remo stay with Ruby in the apartment over her factory. Perhaps proximity could produce the kind of results persuasion could not. His fourteen steamer trunks were moved into a back room of the small apartment and when Remo wasn't listening, Chiun told Ruby that he would get any male child from the relationship, providing it was healthy. The Gonzalezes could keep the females.

Ruby answered that women were really smarter than men and that what Chiun said was a sexist comment. Chiun wanted to know what "sexist" meant because he had heard it often on American television.

"Sexist is thinking women can't do things that men can do," said Ruby.

"I also think water is wet," said Chiun, who wondered if there was a title for that, too. Maybe he was a "wettist."

It took Chiun thirty-two seconds to figure out what had happened that mysterious day when the men disappeared. He explained it to Remo in Korean.

"What he say?" Ruby asked.

"He said it was a slave raid," Remo said.

"Lucius a slave? Lucius never do a lick of work in his life. Neither did anybody else who's gone."

Chiun nodded. He spoke again in Korean.

"Tell him to stop talking funny," said Ruby.

"He says it's not funny. He says you're funny. He says you have funny eyes and a funny nose. He says if we produce a male child, it will have to overcome its ugliness. It will be the ugliest child in the world."

"I know you talk English, Chiun," said Ruby, "so why not talk right."

"You're ugly," said Chiun who was now happy. What he did not mention was that he planned the male child hopefully to be smarter than Remo because Ruby was. He liked her mind. He would match her mind with Remo's body and hopefully start another Master of Sinanju correctly. Without bad habits like talking back. He also didn't mention that he didn't really find Ruby ugly, but he noticed that when he abused her, Remo took her side. And perhaps if he abused her enough, he could drive Remo close enough to her to create the new heir of Sinanju.

97

"Not only was this a slave raid, but I'm sure it was just a demonstration," Chiun said.

"You talk all right when you want to," said Ruby, still miffed at Chiun.

"She's not ugly. She's beautiful," Remo said.

"No flesh," said Chiun.

"You like them fat like that butterball with hair on her forehead back in Korea," said Remo.

"You ain't so good looking," Ruby told Chiun.

"I am trying to carry on a civilized conversation with an ugly person and you descend, girl, to name calling. Name calling is especially vicious from an ugly woman. But I will not indulge you in your baseness. You have enough problems with a face like that." Remo took a half step closer to Ruby. Chiun was pleased.

"Look," said Remo. "Let's stop the name calling and get down to business. Why do you think it's a demonstration, Little Father?"

Chiun nodded. "Can you understand English, child?" he asked Ruby.

"Sure," she said suspiciously.

"I was wondering if you could hear because of those peculiar muffs on the side of your head."

"Ain' nothin' on the side of my head. Those my ears," said Ruby.

"I thought so," said Chiun. "They were too ugly for earmuffs." And then he explained that it was customary in a slave raid before a war to take some of the people of a nation and demonstrate that they could be made into slaves easily. This made the enemy's army even more fearsome.

"But do not worry," Chiun said.

"Why not?" asked Ruby.

98

"I have been thinking of it and the issue of you and Remo might be worthwhile."

"Dammit, we not talking about children," Ruby said. "We talking about Lucius. You want a child, you go to the welfare, they got hundreds of babies. They giving them away."

"But not Remo's. He owes me a son. One male child."

"You want to get it from me, you better be getting Lucius back," Ruby said. "Where we find him?"

"You said you know people all over this part of the country?" Chiun said.

"That's right."

He stopped at a map of the United States hanging on the wall behind a light piece of glass tinted yellow from Mrs. Gonzalez's pipe smoke.

"Where don't you have contacts?" asked Chiun.

"Hardly anyplace," said Ruby.

"Show me," Chiun said.

"That's dumb," Ruby said.

"Show me," Chiun insisted.

He nodded as Ruby jabbed her finger at the map, pointing out states and cities and who her contacts were, as she looked for an area where she didn't have a friend or an acquaintance or someone who owed her a favor.

"What about there?" said Chiun, pointing to the map. "That is one spot you did not mention."

"The great piney woods? Shoot, nobody is there. Nobody goes in and nobody comes out."

Remo smiled at Chiun.

"Ain't nothin' there," said Ruby.

"Even Remo knows," said Chiun.

"Little Father, I don't like these comments

about my intelligence," Remo said. "I may be the only sane one among the three of us and maybe that's why I appear dumb. I don't know. But it's reached its limit. I don't want to hear it again. Enough."

Ruby looked confused. Chiun looked wounded. What had he done? He had held his tongue remarkably, despite the fact that he was surrounded by a gravel-brained white and a black-and-white mixture in a coat of light chocolate with two wounded Brussels sprouts for ears. This he said and he wondered aloud about it all the way to the edge of the great piney woods in Western South Carolina.

He wondered why they were walking in forests like animals when the true civilized assassin worked in cities.

He wondered why, like pack animals, they trudged many miles following obvious footsteps. Signs of an army were unmistakable. The heavily trod ground. The new-made paths where hundreds of men went in one direction.

To Remo and Chiun, the signs were like neon lights saying: this way to armed camp.

Chiun never wanted to say Remo was dumb and he wanted Remo to understand that. It was just that some assassins were assassins and some went on television. It was not up to Chiun, the Master of Sinanju, to say that choosing worthless uncomfortable work was dumb, and choosing wealth and fame and honor was stupid. Chiun was not about to say that. And why was Chiun not about to say that?

"Enough," said Remo. "Are you going to work? I'm going to work. Are you going to talk

100

or are you going to work?" They knew the camp was near because the access routes were more worn. It was like a swelling, on the same principle insurance men discovered when they found most auto accidents occurred within twenty-five miles of the home: It was not because people drove more carelessly near home; it was because they did most of their traveling within that distance.

"I am not saying anything," said Chiun.

"Good," said Remo.

The first guards were several paces away. It was a double man in a set position and long hours had already set into their eyes. And not expecting to see anything down the pine wood path on his oven-hot day, they were not about to spot the Master of the Sinanju and the American who was also of Sinanju—of it, but not from it—so much now of Sinanju that he was indistinguishable from that first assassin so many centuries ago who first set forth from his poor village to bring back sustenance by his killing skills.

It was a traditional Roman camp, square with the command somewhere off to the side, so that if the walls succumbed the center could be used as a formation area for what the Romans did best—maneuver with discipline. Centuries after men stopping using spears and swords and shields, camps were still laid out in squares with the open parade grounds in the center. It made no sense, but Masters of Sinanju knew that most men fought using things they did not understand and so fought badly.

Remo and Chiun were inside the square camp without much difficulty and had an officer over a desk with even less difficulty. The camp was almost deserted. The officer had a replica of a New Hampshire license plate on his desk. The license said "Live Free or Die." The officer was not all that committed to such a strict interpretation of his license plate. Reasonable men were always willing to compromise, especially when one of the reasonable men felt his arms about to leave his shoulders and he didn't feel like going through life, assuming he was going to live through this, with sockets instead of fingers. He also played the piano. He owed it to his piano playing to tell everything.

This was a special unit with special assignments, special pay, and special discipline. Its commander was a Lieutenant Colonel Bleech. The code words for the day were . . .

"I'm not interested in code words, Captain, and not in who runs this outfit. I'm looking for an incredibly lazy, useless person."

"My company isn't here anymore. They went with Colonel Bleech, but no one knows where they went."

This worthless person isn't in your company. His name is Lucius Jackson."

But before the captain could speak, Chiun raised a finger. In Korean, he told Remo, "This is not a slave place. The slaves are not here."

CHAPTER EIGHT

It had to have been a military operation, thought Harold Smith as he bought a used golf ball from the pro shop at the Folcroft Hills Golf Club. He spent three minutes going through the twenty-five-cent jar, looking for a Titleist. He did not like to play with cheap golf balls.

He finally found one without a cut in the cover, but with a deep crescent crease that made the ball look like a white "Smile" button. With dimples.

As he cleaned the ball in the washer on the first tee, he asked himself where a military operation might have been launched from. The raid on Norfolk had not been done by any of the regular military units. He had known that. All troop movements from anywhere to anywhere were monitored by CURE's computers. But still there had been uniformed men in large number. A large force. And a large force meant training and training meant a base.

The caddy watched with barely disguised disgust as Smith finished cleaning the used ball. He had caddied for Smith before and, to tell the truth, he was not all that anxious to work four hours for a fifty-cent tip. When they had seen Smith walking from the clubhouse toward the

first tee, all the other caddies had made themselves scarce. This one had been the slowest and
so he had been nailed. He cursed his luck. Other
people caught movie stars, politicians, enter-
tainers to caddy for. He got "Tightwad" Smith,
and it was the nature of the man that the caddy
would never even catch a hint that he was being
privileged to caddy for one of the three or four
most powerful men in the world.

Even if it was just for fifty cents.

Smith was oblivious to his reputation among
the caddies. He had long ago decided that men
paid good money for the right to walk around a
golf course, so why should a caddy decide that he
should be paid money to walk around the same
course? The only untidy factor in the equation
was the golf bag. The caddy had to carry the bag
of clubs. This constituted work and was therefore
worth something. Smith figured it at about three
cents a hole. That was fifty-four cents. Rounding
it off to the lowest nickel made fifty cents. It did
not bother him that other golfers tipped their
caddies four and five dollars a bag. If they
wanted to waste their money, that was their
business.

Smith breathed deeply of the still chilly
morning air, laced with salt from the nearby
sound, and felt vaguely guilty about being on the
golf course. He had once played golf regularly,
once a week without fail, but in recent years, the
work of CURE had multiplied like cancer cells
and he found it impossible to scrape together the
time away from his desk.

But this day he had decided just to go out and
do it. There were a lot of things to think about

and he had to be able to think without interruption. This was his justification.

Remo had vanished; Chiun had vanished with him. CURE's killer arm was no more and while Remo had been threatening and trying to quit ever since he'd been recruited, this time there was a reality to it that disturbed Smith. For without an enforcement arm, CURE would be nothing, have nothing to distinguish it from the laundry ticket of government agencies, all tripping over each other, all gathering the same intelligence, and all just sitting on it because they were afraid to act on it.

And there was the raid in Norfolk. He would have liked to pick up the telephone and tell Remo to get down there. But there was no longer any Remo to call.

He was worried and, as he carefully placed his ball on the white wooden tee that some other golfer had casually dropped, Smith hoped that his worry would not affect his golf game. Assuming he had a golf game left. He prided himself that he had once played the game well.

The first hole was a straight-away 385-yard par four. A pro would play it with a 240-yard drive, a 140-yard seven iron, and two putts.

Harold Smith cranked up and swung at the ball. He hit it clean, right on the screws, straight down the center of the fairway. The ball hit 135 yards out and rolled for 40 more yards before stopping.

The drive almost brought a smile to Smith's face. His game was still intact. Worry had not ruined it. He politely handed his driver to the caddy and walked off after his ball. He knew how he would play the round. He would not par a hole, but he would not double-bogey a hole either. He would shoot every hole in exactly one over par. He would two putt every green.

Par for this course was 72; he would shoot 90. He always shot 90, and, if he had wanted to, he could have mailed his scores in. Ninety seemed to him a perfectly good score. Consistency. The idea of hitting great shots, miracle shots, and using them to balance off your occasional bad shots never occurred to him. He liked it the way he did it. Everything straight down the middle.

But what about Norfolk?

A military operation. There had to be a training base. But where?

He used a fairway wood for his second shot and hit it straight toward the green. It traveled with roll another 130 yards. He was 110 yards from the green.

Without being asked, the caddy handed Smith a four iron, which he swung and laced his ball onto the green twelve feet from the hole. He putted to within a foot, then dropped the short second putt and scored a five.

Sullenly, the caddy took the ball from the cup, replaced the flagstick and handed the ball toward Smith.

But Smith was not looking at the caddy. He was staring off at the trees and dense woods bordering both sides of the narrow first fairway. An idea was trickling through.

"Son," Smith told the caddy. "I've decided not to play anymore today."

The pimple-faced boy sighed and Smith took it mistakenly for disappointment.

"Now obviously I can't tip you the full fifty cents because you only caddied one hole," Smith said.

The boy nodded.

"What do you think would be fair?" Smith asked.

The boy shrugged. He had already decided that he would pay Smith up to two dollars, just to be rid of him, so he could get back to the caddy's shack and maybe get a paying customer.

Smith looked at the ball in the caddy's hand.

"I just paid twenty-five cents for that ball," Smith said. "Suppose you keep it and we call it even?"

The caddy looked at the ball. The crescent slice on it seemed to smile up at him.

"Gee, Doctor Smith, that's wonderful. I can probably resell it again and make ten, maybe even fifteen, cents."

"Just what I thought," said Smith. "At ten cents, that would average out to a dollar-eighty for eighteen holes. At fifteen cents, it would be two dollars and seventy cents."

Smith paused, and appeared to be calculating. For a frightened moment, the caddy wondered if Smith was going to want him to split the proceeds of the resale. Smith was thinking about exactly that. Then he shook his head firmly. "No," he said. "You keep it all."

"Thank you, Doctor Smith."

"Think nothing of it," Smith said. He walked off the green back toward the clubhouse.

"I'll see you next week," he called over his shoulder.

He did not hear the caddy groan behind him, then turn and throw the ball into the woods.

After the ten-minute drive back to his office in the old sanitarium building, Smith surprised his secretary polishing her nails on company time. He cocked an eyebrow at Miss Purvish, who looked as if she would be glad to drink the nail polish, anything to make it disappear.

"What happened to playing golf?" she managed to ask, hastily capping the bottle of polish.

"It's too nice a day to play golf," said Smith. "Don't disturb me unless it is absolutely necessary."

Inside his office, Smith sat behind the large, desk, his back to the one-way windows that looked out over the Sound, and began planning.

A military maneuver meant a military installation somewhere. And a military installation meant buildings and plumbing and access and water lines and sewerage.

Smith pressed a button. A panel opened in his desk and a computer console rose in front of him, like a silent servant awaiting instructions.

Smith asked it for the number of areas within a two-hundred-and-fifty-mile radius of Norfolk, large enough and isolated enough to hold a secret military installation. It took seven minutes for the computer to scan its memory maps and tapes and report back that there were seven hundred and forty-six possible locations.

Smith groaned silently. The task was monumental. Then he took a deep breath. One bite at a time. How many of these areas within the last year, had had extensive building done on them he asked the computer.

The computer dug deep into the mass of miscellaneous information buried in its tapes.

Forty-three, it responded, over the television monitor on Smith's desk.

In how many of the forty-three areas had there been sewerage construction on a scale too big for private homes?

As he waited for the computer to answer, Smith idly punched up the list of those kidnapped in Norfolk. He saw the name of Lucius Jackson and next of kin, R. Gonzalez. The name jogged a faint memory switch in the back of his head. R. Gonzalez? R. Gonzalez?

The computer began to clack almost silently as an answer appeared on the television screen.

There were three areas that fit Smith's requirements. One in Virginia, one in North Carolina, and one in South Carolina.

Smith leaned back in his chair and thought for a moment. A secret installation. Which of the three, if any, had no record of road construction in the last year?

The computer answered quickly. The piney woods of South Carolina.

That would be it, Smith thought. For a secret installation, they would not build access roads. He double-checked the information, and asked the computer if, in the last year, there had been an increase in helicopter flights over the piney woods area in South Carolina.

A six hundred-percent increase, the computer told him instantly.

Smith arranged his mouth in what, for him, passed for a smile. The helicopter flights nailed it down. Without roads, they would be moving their men and materials in and out by helicopter. That was it. The piney woods of South Carolina.

He was about to erase the information he had just obtained when he paused, remembered, and asked the machine for a readout on R. Gonzalez, Norfolk, Virginia.

The machine replied in twenty seconds. "R. Gonzalez. Ruby Jackson Gonzalez. Twenty-three. Wig Manufacturer, owner of two real estate agencies, director of four banks, Triple A from Dun and Bradstreet. Subject former CIA agent, recently released from service. Last assignment, Baqia, where came into contact with agency personnel."

Smith gave a triumphant hiss, punched the buttons that cleared the computer's memory of the questions he had asked, and lowered it back into the desk.

Ruby Gonzalez. He had spoken to her when Remo and Chiun were in trouble on the Baqian mission. She had saved their lives.

And she was involved in this; her brother had been seized. She wasn't Remo or Chiun, but she might be able to help.

Miss Purvish answered the telephone as soon as Smith picked it up.

"Get me a ticket as soon as possible to Norfolk, Virginia," he said.

"Right away, Doctor. Round trip?"

"Yes."

"Right away, sir."

She hung up as Smith replaced the phone. He

110

thought of something else and quickly picked up the receiver again.

"Yes sir," said Miss Purvish.

"Make that tourist," Smith said.

CHAPTER NINE

The old black woman wore a red bandanna around her head and a house dress that dropped in a straight line, unbroken by any hint of human curve, from neck to feet, encased in plush bedroom slippers at least four sizes too big.

The pipe she was smoking gave off toxic fumes, the like of which he had not smelled since commandoes under his leadership exploded a German cordite factory in Norway in 1944.

"I am looking for Ruby Gonzalez," Smith said.

"C'mon in," said Ruby's mother.

She led Smith into the parlor of the small apartment and motioned Smith to the chair opposite her blue rocker. He sat down in the overstuffed seat, and sank for what seemed like a full three seconds before stopping.

"Lemme see yo' hands," Mrs. Gonzalez said.

"I'm looking for Ruby. She's your daughter, I believe."

"Ah knows who my daughter is," said Mrs. Gonzalez. "Show me yo' hands."

Smith struggled back up to the edge of the chair and extended his hands before him. Maybe she was going to tell his fortune. The gaunt black woman took his hands in hers in a grip like a

112

vise. She looked at the palms, then the fingers, then turned them over and looked at the backs, then released them as if they were the most no-account hands she had ever seen.

"Don' see nothing special about them hands."

"Why should there be something special about them?"

"Listen, you. You be here to get Lucius back or not?"

"I came here to see Ruby. Your daughter."

"You not the man who gonna get Lucius back?"

Smith felt as if the old woman was going to tell him something important.

"Perhaps," he said. "What did Ruby say?"

"Ruby, she be watching the television and she see these hands, and she say, like, that's him, that's him, he gonna get Lucius back and they be white hands and I think they be yours 'cause all white hands look alike."

Hands? Hands. What was she talking about?

"So you be the man or not?" Mrs. Gonzalez asked.

"I'm going to try to get Lucius back," Smith said.

"Okay. Befo' Ruby gets home, I wants to talk to yo' about that."

"Yes?" asked Smith.

"Why you just not let Lucius be where he be?"

"You mean not bring him back?"

The old woman nodded her head. "Ruby miss him a little bit now," she said. "But that not last long. And when she sees how good we does without him, she be happy. He be about the most worthlessest boy ah ever see."

Smith nodded.

"When will Ruby be back?" he asked.

"What time's it?"

Smith glanced at his watch. "Two-thirty."

"She be back before six."

"Are you sure?"

"Sure. That my supper time and that girl never miss fixing my supper."

"I'll be back, Mrs. Gonzalez," Smith said.

"C'mon, c'mon, step on it," Ruby said. "I got to get home to cook Mama's dinner."

"I'm going eighty-five now," Remo said.

"Go faster," Ruby said. She folded her arms across her bosom and stared out the front windshield of the white Lincoln Continental.

"Silence up there," commanded Chiun from the back seat, where he sat by himself, toying with the dials of a CB radio set built into the floor of the vehicle.

"Don't break that radio," Remo said.

"It's all right," Ruby said. "I got that for Mama when I take her on drives. She like to talk a lot and I don't like to listen all that much. This way she talks to somebody else."

Chiun found the "on" switch and the radio squawked into the car, filling it with sound. Ruby reached over the seat and turned down the volume. She handed Chiun the microphone.

"So now you see why we gotta talk to that tired-ass boss of yours, that Doctor Smith," said Ruby.

"No, I don't see," said Remo.

"'Cause we gotta find out where Lucius was

taken. And he's got a better chance of knowing than we got," Ruby said.

"Sorry. No more. I'm done with that gang."

From the back, Chiun called, "This is very interesting, Remo. This device is obviously hooked up to an insane asylum. I keep getting talked to by idiots who have some kind of handles attached to them."

"A handle's a name that they call themselves," said Ruby, and to Remo, "You've got to do it."

"No."

"For me," said Ruby.

"Especially not for you."

"Will you two be quiet?" said Chiun. "Somebody here knows me. He says he is my good buddy."

"Then for Lucius," Ruby said.

"The hell with Lucius."

"Lucius never do nothing to you."

"Only because I never met him," Remo said.

"He's my brother. You got to call that Doctor Smith."

"No."

"Then I'll call him," said Ruby.

"You call him and I'll leave." Remo glanced into the rear-view mirror. Chiun had a broad smile on his face and was turning to the left, pressing his face against the window, then leaning across the seat to press his face against the right window, then turning in the seat to smile out the back window.

"Chiun, why are you smiling?" Remo asked.

"Some one of my good buddies told me that breaker, breaker, picture taker is here and I am smiling for my picture."

"Picture taker?" said Remo. "What's that mean?"

"That means you going too fast," Ruby screeched. "Slow down."

Too late. From behind the wall of a bridge overpass, a hidden police car pulled out into the traffic lane, flicked on its siren and flashing lights, and started after the speeding Remo.

"You just told me I was going too slow," Remo said.

"Not when there's a cop around. Picture taker, that's radar by the cops. They was warning you on that radio," Ruby said. "Now we gets arrested."

"Not exactly yet," said Remo as he tromped on the accelerator.

The trooper disappeared far behind as Remo went over the second hill in the road at one twenty-five, took an exit onto a side road to avoid troopers who would try to pull him off up ahead, and slowed down to ninety for the rest of the trip into Norfolk.

When they pulled up in front of Ruby's wig factory, Chiun was shouting in Korean into the CB microphone.

"What's he saying?" Ruby asked.

"He's telling somebody that if he ever meets him, he will crack him like an egg on the sidewalk," said Remo.

"Why he say that?"

"I think somebody called him ratchet jaw," Remo said.

The taste of salt hung in the air on Jefferson Street like a daytime fog, as Chiun followed Remo and Ruby out of the car.

116

From a small restaurant across the street, Smith saw them, left a nickel tip on the table, and walked quickly outside.

"Remo," he called.

The three turned to look at the man in the gray suit coming across the street.

"Who's that?" Ruby said.

"As if you didn't know, fink."

"Chiun, who's that?" Ruby asked.

"That is the Emperor Smith," Chiun hissed.

"That's him? He don't look like much," said Ruby.

"And when you get to know him, he's even less," Remo said. "What are you doing here, Smitty?"

"I'm looking for Lucius Jackson," said Smith. "Are you Ruby Gonzalez?"

Ruby nodded.

"I think we might find out something about your brother's disappearance in the piney woods in South Carolina," Smith said.

"We was just there," Ruby said.

"And?"

"Wait just a minute," Remo said. "Smitty, we aren't working for you anymore. What are all these questions?"

"If we're both trying to do the same thing, doesn't it make sense to do it together?" asked Smith.

"No," said Remo. "I'm leaving."

He took a step away but was stopped by Chiun who let loose a flood of Korean words. Remo listened, then turned back to Smith.

"All right. But you're not in charge here. I am."

117

Smith nodded.

"We were too late to the piney woods. There was some kind of army there but they moved out. Nobody knows where. But Lucius and the others weren't there at all and that's all we know."

"An army," Smith said.

"That's right," said Remo.

"An army should leave traces," said Smith.

"Good. You sniff 'em out," Remo said, "and let me know what you find out." He walked into the wig factory. Smith followed him.

"What'd you tell him to make him change his mind and stay?" Ruby asked Chiun.

"It is not important," said Chiun.

"I want to know."

"I told him that if he left now, he would not discharge his debt to you for saving his life, and he would forever be subject to listen to your squawking screeching voice, yelling in his ears."

Ruby patted Chiun on the shoulder. "That was a good thing to tell him."

"And true," said Chiun who still had not figured out a way to get Remo and Ruby together to create a new baby for Sinanju.

CHAPTER TEN

"Fourteen college buses, spaced at five-minute intervals, have been seen riding along Route 675 toward Pennsylvania," Smith said, as he hung up the telephone.

"So what?" said Remo. "They're going to a baseball game."

"They're from Marywether College, Allenby School, Bartlett University, Southern Jersey State, Northern School of the Atlantic, and Saint Olaf's."

"All right," said Remo. "A cricket game. So what?"

"So there are no colleges by those names in the United States," Smith said.

"Can we get a fix on where they're going?" Ruby asked.

"It's in the works. They'll be monitored," Smith said.

"Time to move out," Ruby said. "Be back tomorrow, Mama. Iffen you get hungry, you send somebody out from downstairs to get you something. We going for Lucius."

"I be all right, chile," said Mrs. Gonzalez, swaying back and forth in her rocking chair. She looked at Smith and shook her head no, trying to catch his eye, still believing that he was the one with the power to decide whether or not to bring back Lucius and trying to convince him not to.

Driving out of Norfolk, Chiun fiddled with the CB radio.

"How do you like retirement?" Smith asked Remo.

"A lot better than I liked working for you," Remo said.

"Have you given a thought to what you'll live on?" Smith asked. "You know that you just can't keep charging things to me anymore."

"Don't you worry about me," Remo said. "I'm going to be a television star. And when those residuals come pouring in, I'm going to live like a king forever."

"You retired," Ruby said to Remo. "You don't look like the retiring type."

"I quit," said Remo. "Too many bodies without names, too much death."

"Remo," said Smith sharply. Remo met his eyes in the rear-view mirror. Smith glanced toward Ruby.

"Don't worry about it, Smitty. She knows more about the organization than you could guess. If you didn't find us, she wanted us to find you."

"You're remarkably well-informed," Smith said to Ruby.

"I keep my ears open," Ruby said.

"Which is hard when you have ears like Brussels sprouts," Chiun said.

A squawking came over the radio and Chiun said hello.

"What's the handle, good buddy?" a voice asked.

"I tell you as I tell the others. People do not have handles."

"What do you call yourself?"

"What do I call myself or what do others call me?"

"What can I call you?" the voice asked. The accent was dry Oklahoma and Remo marveled that no matter where you heard a CB-er talk, they all sounded as if they lived in a tarpaper shack on the outskirts of Tulsa.

"I call myself modest, kind, humble, and generous," Chiun said. "Others call me glorious, enlightened, wonder of the ages, and worshipful master."

"Quite a handle. Suppose I just call you modest?"

"Just call me Master, as befits my character. Did I ever tell you, medium tolerable buddy, that I used to work for a secret government agency?"

Smith groaned and pushed his head against the corner of the seat.

Lt. Colonel Wendell Bleech was in the first of the fourteen buses spread out along the highway. He sat behind the driver, a headset over his ears, monitoring any calls that might be coming to him from home base.

The fifty men on his bus were dressed in jeans and T-shirts, and Bleech had relaxed discipline enough so that they were allowed to talk to each other. But not too loud.

His top lieutenant slid into the seat next to Bleech.

"Finally getting this show on the road," he said, in as much a question as a statement.

121

"Yessir," Bleech said. "Men ready?"

"You know that better than I do, Colonel. They're as ready as we can make them."

Bleech nodded and looked out the window at the countryside rolling by.

"We didn't do a thing that they couldn't do in the regular army," he said. "If they wanted to."

The lieutenant grunted agreement.

"Twenty years I watched," Bleech said. "The army going downhill. Salaries going up. Morale down. Turning it into a country club. Civil rights for dog soldiers. All volunteers so treat 'em with kid gloves. And all the while I was thinking, give me this army for six months I could turn 'em around, shape 'em up, and make a real army out of them. Like Patton had. Like Custer had."

The lieutenant nodded. "Like Pershing," he offered.

Bleech shook his head. "Well, not exactly like Pershing. You know where he got that Blackjack nickname from?"

"No."

"He used to run a black outfit in the army. They called him Nigger Jack at first. No, scratch Pershing. But they never gave me the chance and then they all got their little asses in an uproar 'cause some civilians got shot in Nam, and here I was, all I wanted to do was make the army good, and I was getting thrown out on my ear."

"Soft," the lieutenant said. "Everybody's soft today."

"Then I got this chance, and these are the best troops I ever saw. Best conditioned, the best trained, the best disciplined. I'd march them into hell."

"And they'd follow you, sure enough," the lieutenant said.

Bleech turned and smiled at his lieutenant and clapped a friendly hand on his shoulder. "Someday," he said, "when this country gets itself all straightened out, they're going to strike medals for us. But until then we got to get our reward just from the doing."

His earphones crackled and he raised a hand toward the lieutenant for silence. He swung the small mike down from its anchor on top of the earphones.

"White Fox One here," he said. "Go ahead."

He listened intently for almost a minute, then said briskly, "Got it. Good work."

He snapped the microphone back up atop the headset and the lieutenant looked at him quizzically.

"Trouble?" he asked.

"We had visitors at the camp."

"Yeah?"

"They didn't learn anything there, but they must have gotten something somewhere else. They've been seen coming from Norfolk, following us along this road."

"Following us?"

"Looks that way."

"Who are they?" the lieutenant asked.

"Don't know. Three men and a woman."

"What do we do?"

A small smile spread slowly across Bleech's face. It made him look like a Halloween pumpkin.

"We'll give them a welcome."

For over two hours, Chiun had been trying to

123

convince everybody on the CB's forty channels that they should be silent for exactly seventy-five minutes so that he could recite one of the shorter works of Ung poetry. No one had paid any attention to his demands for silence and as Remo, following a report Smith had received from a roadside phone call, turned onto a dirt road near Gettysburg, Pennsylvania, Chiun was yelling threats and insults into the CB in Korean.

Hidden in the hills bordering the road a half mile away, three soldiers saw the white Continental kick up a puff of dust as it came off the pavement into the narrow road.

"He always like this when he travels?" Ruby asked Remo, jerking her thumb toward Chiun.

"Only when we're going someplace he doesn't want to go."

"What's he saying now?" Ruby asked. Smith sat up nervously. Whenever Chiun spoke Korean, Smith worried that he was giving away the last few secrets that remained to the United States Government.

Remo cocked an ear. "He is telling that moderately acceptable buddy that the only difference between him and cow droppings is that cow droppings can be burned in a fire."

Another voice squawked and Chiun squawked back. "And he's telling that one," Remo translated, "that he should drink sheep dip."

Remo bumped along the pocked dirt road in the soft-sprung Continental while the screeching continued from the back seat and Ruby covered her ears with her hands to muffle the noise.

Suddenly, Chiun was silent. Ruby turned in her seat to see what had stopped the noise in the car, but as she turned, Chiun dove past her, across the front seat and grabbed the steering wheel from Remo with his left hand.

He gave a sharp yank and the car swerved to the right, almost at a ninety-degree angle, moving off the narrow roadway and toward a tree. At the last split instant before it hit the tree, Chiun forced the wheel back in the other direction.

Remo looked at Chiun, his mouth open to question him, when there were two explosive thumps, in close succession, in the roadway behind them. The car was hit with flying rocks and dirt and clouds of dust and acrid smoke swirled up on the road.

"Mortars," Remo yelled. He tromped down heavily on the gas pedal, took the wheel back, and sped down the road.

Chiun nodded, as if satisfied, and slid back to his seat. Smith was looking through the rear window, as the dust cleared, at the two holes in the roadway, each the size of a beer barrel.

Remo began to let the car slow down.

"Do not reduce speed yet," said Chiun. "There is another to come."

"How you know that?" asked Ruby.

"Because good things always come in threes," Chiun hissed. As Ruby watched, he seemed to narrow the focus of his eyes, as if staring at a point only inches in front of his nose, then he looked up and said sharply, "Steer left, Remo. Left."

Remo swerved the car sharply to the left and slammed the gas pedal down into passing gear. The car's nose lifted and it careened down the road. There was an explosion behind them that lifted the right side of the car up off its wheels for a moment, but Remo easily pulled the car back under control.

Chiun opened the rear window on his side and listened intently for a few seconds.

."That is all," he said. Without a pause, he picked up the CB microphone again and resumed screaming into it in high-pitched Korean.

"How'd he do that?" Ruby asked.

"He heard them," Remo said.

"I didn't hear them," said Ruby.

"That's 'cause you've got ears like Brussels sprouts."

"How could he hear them when he was yelling all the time into that radio?" Ruby asked.

"Why not?" said Remo. "He knows what he's yelling into the radio; he doesn't have to listen to that. So he was listening to everything else and he heard the mortars."

"Just like that?"

"Just like that," Remo said, knowing it would never satisfy her. The art of Sinanju was simple and people wanted complexity. There was no complexity in telling the simple truth—that Sinanju taught a person to use his body the way it should be used.

"If you're so smart, how come you didn't hear them?" asked Ruby.

"Chiun hears better than I do," Remo said.

"Silence," thundered Chiun from the rear. "Since I hear so well, do you realize what an affront to me is your constant yammering. Be still, the two of you. I am preparing to deliver my Ung poetry."

"Sorry, Little Father," Remo said. "Have to

wait a while." He rolled the car off the road and into a small stand of trees. "This is the end of the line." He looked around to Smith.

"Their mortar men will be reporting back that they missed us, so they'll be waiting. We'll have to go on foot. Smitty, you and Ruby take the car and go back."

"Bull," said Ruby.

"She has a good heart, this one," Chiun said. "She will make brave sons."

"Cut it out, Chiun," said Remo. "You'll just slow us down, Smitty. We passed a gas station back on the left about a mile. You go back there and wait for us. We'll be back as soon as we get a fix on this thing."

Smith thought a moment, then nodded. "All right. I can make use of that telephone there, too," he said.

Remo and Chiun slipped from the car and Ruby drove away. As soon as she got onto the road, she glanced up into her rear-view mirror. Remo and Chiun were gone, nowhere to be seen.

Ruby kicked up dust coming around a curve, narrowly missing one of the mortar craters, before a long straight run that led back to the main road. As she came around the curve, she jammed on the brakes. Parked across the road was an ol-ive-drab army-type truck, but with no military markings.

Four men with automatic weapons jumped toward the front of the car as Ruby braked, and pressed the barrels of their weapons against the glass. Ruby threw the Continental in reverse and looked up quickly into the rear-view mirror. Three more men were standing behind the car, their weapons pressed against the glass, aimed at her head and Smith's.

"Better stop," Smith said.

"Sheeit," said Ruby.

A man wearing sergeant's stripes on his khakis hopped lightly down from the cab of the truck.

"All right, both of you, get out of there." He elaborately opened the rear door for Smith. "Out," he said.

Then he opened the front passenger's door, leaned in and smiled at Ruby. His teeth were yellowed with tobacco stains and his accent was deep, deep Alabama South.

"You too, nigger," he said.

"Well, if it ain't the Koo Koo Klucks," said Ruby.

At the top of a small hill, Remo looked around and recognized where he was. Stretching out before him were the rolling hills of southern Pennsylvania, dotted with monuments, statues, and small buildings.

"This is Gettysburg," Remo said wonderingly. "There's Cemetery Ridge. And there's Culps Hill."

"What is this Gettysburg?" asked Chiun.

"It was a battlefield," Remo said.

"In a war?"

"Yes."

"What war?"

"The Civil War."

"That was the war over slavery," Chiun said.

Remo nodded. "And now we're looking for another army that's trying to keep slavery alive."

"We will not find it on top of this hill," Chiun said.

Below the heel, in a small clearing, Remo found three small dents in the ground left by the triangular base of the field mortar.

"One of them was here, Chiun," he said.

Chiun nodded. "They expected us," he said.

"Why?"

"Because this lowland spot commands no view of the road. There were three shells fired at us. One of them must have been able to sight our vehicle and by radio told the others when to fire. But they were already targeted on a roadway they could not see. They expected us."

Chiun pointed through the trees. "And they went this way."

"Then let's go join the army," Remo said.

In the clearing behind one of the small hills outside Gettysburg, a military field camp had been set up. The clearing was bordered by military trucks and the buses that had brought the men from their South Carolina base. Parked in a corner of the field was Ruby Gonzalez's white Continental.

Only one tent had been erected, a fifteen-foot square standup wall tent that served as Colonel Bleech's command post and sleeping quarters, while he waited further orders.

Natty and round in dress gabardines, his riding trousers bloused neatly inside his highly polished boots, Bleech slapped his riding crop against his right thigh as he looked at Smith and Ruby. They were guarded by the sergeant with the yellow teeth and three soldiers carrying automatic weapons.

Behind them, sitting on the ground watching,

were five-hundred young troopers, the main body of Bleech's army. They had been hastily turned out when Ruby and Smith were brought in, and as they marched in to sit on the ground in neat rows, Ruby glanced at them. Crackers, she thought. Deep South, shit-kicking crackers without a brain in their little racist heads.

Bleech, conscious of the need to make a good impression on his men, marched briskly back and forth in front of Ruby and Smith. Ruby yawned and covered her mouth with the back of her hand.

"All right," Bleech growled. "Who are you?" His voice carried loudly over the clearing and hung in the air. The troops sat hushed, watching the scene.

"We from the town hall," said Ruby. "We come to look at your parade permit."

Bleech fixed her with narrow eyes. "We'll see how long your sense of humor lasts," he said. "And you?" He turned to Smith.

"I have nothing to say to you," said Smith.

Bleech nodded, then spoke over Ruby's and Smith's heads to his troops.

"Men, look well. Know the face of the enemy. These are spies." He paused to let it sink in. "Traitors and spies. And in wartime, and this is wartime because everything we cherish as Americans is being warred upon by people like this, in wartime there is only one penalty for spies and traitors." He stopped again and let his eyes roam from one end of the clearing to the other. "Death," he intoned.

"You gonna show us your parade permit or not?" asked Ruby.

"We'll see if you have so much of a sense of hu-

130

mor in front of a firing squad," Bleech said. "But first you're going to tell us who you are."

"Don't hold your breath, honkey," said Ruby.

"We will see." Bleech nodded to the sergeant who moved up close behind Ruby then slammed his hands against her shoulder blades, shoving her forward. She stumbled toward Bleech who turned his lead-tipped riding crop forward. Its weighted butt end buried itself deep into Ruby's stomach. She let her breath out with a heavy *oomph* and fell to the ground in the dust.

Bleech laughed. Smith growled, a growl of simple animal anger, and lunged forward at the colonel. Bleech raised the riding crop over his head and swung its weighted end at Smith's skull. But as it whooshed toward him, Smith ducked. The crop passed over his head and Smith came up with a hard New England fist into Bleech's fleshy nose. The colonel grabbed at his nose with his free hand. The four soldiers guarding Ruby and Smith jumped forward and bore Smith to the ground with their weight. One zealous private slammed the butt of his rifle down into Smith's right shoulder.

Ignoring the pain, Smith looked up from the ground at Bleech, holding his bloody nose, and recognized in him all the little tinpot tyrants and bullies he had hated all his life. "Brave when you hit women," he sneered.

Bleech took his hand away from his face. A river of blood ran down from his nose to his fleshy lips.

"Restrain that man. He will get his. *After* the pickaninny."

He reached down, grabbed Ruby by the hair, and yanked her up to her feet.

"But first you." He turned her head and shouted to his men. "Memorize this. It is the face of the enemy." As he spoke, droplets of blood splashed out from his mouth and spattered Ruby's shirt.

No one saw them. No one heard them. A pair of sentries was posted at each of the four corners of the field, their sole duty to insure that no one sneaked into the main area of the camp.

But none of them saw Remo and Chiun.

The two men moved into the compound and then went silently through the back wall of Bleech's tent. Hidden by the darkness from the hundreds of pairs of eyes outside, they saw Bleech pull Ruby up to her feet by her hair. She let herself be dragged up. When her face was level with Bleech's she hacked and spat into his bloodied face.

Chiun nodded. "She is courageous, that one. She will give me a very good son. Through you, of course," he added quickly.

"Forget it," said Remo. He stopped talking as the enraged Bleech pulled his lead riding crop back in his right hand to smash into Ruby's temple. As he extended it behind him, Remo's hand flashed out of the doorway opening of the tent and yanked the crop from Bleech's hand.

The colonel let go of Ruby and spun toward the tent. Remo stepped out into the bright sunshine.

"Hi, guys," he said.

He waved lightly to the five-hundred troops sitting on the ground. They buzzed among themselves, unable to keep still any longer.

"What's this all about?"

"Who's this guy?"

"Bleech'll do a number on him."

"He can't be all there, coming here like this."

Bleech stared at Remo, then reached for the automatic holstered at his side. Remo's hand moved again, and Bleech heard the rip of leather as his holster was neatly excised from his belt and went flying twenty feet away.

"That any way to say hello?" asked Remo.

The sergeant and three soldiers behind Smith had their guns out now. The sergeant had an ugly .45 aimed at Remo's belly; the three privates had their automatic rifles aimed at Remo.

"That's enough," the sergeant said.

Ruby looked around at Remo imploringly. Remo winked.

He turned to the four soldiers. "You're next," he said.

The sergeant extended his gun arm, taking dead aim on Remo's belt buckle.

And then, like the earth ripping open during an earthquake, there was a loud high screeching. The soldiers turned their eyes toward the sound. A small yellow hand with long fingernails protruded through the wall of Bleech's tent. Like a knife, it slashed down toward the ground, and then through the ripped and fluttering canvas came Chiun, Master of Sinanju.

The sergeant wheeled with his gun, but Chiun's yellow robes swirled around him as he moved from the tent. The sergeant's finger squeezed on the gun, but before it fired, Chiun's hand covered the gun. The sergeant could feel the trigger guard being squeezed up behind his index finger, stopping the trigger from being depressed. He felt the crunching of bones, as the tiny yellow hand squeezed, and realized that his bones were being mashed, melted into the automatic as the pressure of Chiun's hand welded the cold steel into his warm living flesh. And there was the pain. The sergeant gave an ear-piercing scream and fell in a crumpled heap, the automatic stuck in his hand as if it had been nailed to it.

The three soldiers alongside him were bare-faced, pimply boys. They watched in terror as the sergeant fell.

They looked at Chiun.

"Fire, you bastards," yelled Bleech.

"Up yours," said one of the soldiers. He dropped his weapon and ran. The other two looked confused.

"I said fire," Bleech hollered.

The two men made the last mistakes of their young lives. They lowered their rifles to their waists, wheeled toward Chiun, and squeezed the triggers. The automatic weapons fired a loud *rat-tat-tat* that tore through the canvas of the tent. Then they fired no more, as their rifles went through their bellies and out their backs, not even slowing down at the spinal column.

They went down, slowly, like jello molds melting away under a heat lamp.

Next to them, the sergeant lay blubbering, trying to disentangle the steel of his automatic from the flesh of his hand.

Bleech looked at the carnage, turned, and tried to run. But Remo slipped his hand into the back of the colonel's Sam Browne belt and held him tight. Bleech's legs moved to run, but he made no progress and, to the five-hundred soldiers, he looked like a cartoon character trying to run over an ice patch and expending heavy labor to no result.

They laughed.

Bleech heard them. Laughing. At a soldier, a career man, a man who had stood for his country when the commies and the pinkos and the lefties and the radicals were trying to destroy it.

"Don't laugh," he screamed.

They laughed harder with that sure young man's sense of knowing when the gang has a new leader.

"All right," Remo said. "Playtime's over. Who runs this operation?"

Bleech gathered his breath as Remo pulled him close by his belt. "Men," he shouted. "You'll see now how a soldier dies when he must." To Remo he said "You'll find out nothing from me."

But nothing in Bleech's experience or training had prepared him for this pain. Remo pinched his left ear lobe between his thumb and index finger and squeezed.

"Who's the leader?" Remo said again.

"Baisley DePauw," Bleech said instantly. And Remo released his ear and the pain gave way to shame that he had cracked so quickly, talked so easily, and his soldiers were laughing aloud now at him, and the shame and anger filled Colonel Bleech's head like a hot red liquid and he scrambled across the ground, found his holster, and pulled out the automatic weapon from it. As he turned to fire, Ruby dove toward the ground,

135

came up with an automatic rifle and squeezed one round neatly into Colonel Bleech's forehead.

He dropped like wet dirty socks.

The troops stopped laughing.

Ruby walked over and nudged Bleech with her toe. Like a cotton packed medicine ball, he rolled over smoothly, dead.

Ruby looked at Remo. "I been wanting to hit that sucker since we got here."

Remo looked at the seated soldiers who just stared at him, frightened, confused, not knowing what to do.

He pointed to Colonel Bleech. "That's it, boys. Your master race. Now get on your buses and go home. This army's been discharged."

The sunlight glinted off the hard planes of Remo's face and the shadows made his deepset dark eyes look like pools of death.

"Go home," he repeated.

None of the soldiers moved; none stirred. It had all happened too fast and they had trouble digesting it.

Remo picked up Bleech's heavy Sam Browne belt, two and a half inches of thick grain leather. He held it in his two hands then, without seeming effort, pulled his hands apart, slowly, almost casually.

As the soldiers watched, the leather ripped apart, the two halves trailing dry stringy strands.

"Go home," Remo said again. "Now!"

One recruit stood at the end of the first row.

"Men. Ah think we better haul ass out of heah."

It turned into a rout, the young soldiers struggling to see who would be first on the bus.

Remo nudged the groaning sergeant with his toe.

"And take your garbage with you," he called.

He looked at Smith, who was holding his right shoulder.

"What's wrong with your arm, Smitty?" he asked.

"Nothing. I fell," Smith said.

CHAPTER ELEVEN

"Look at this, Remo."

A complimentary copy of the *Southern Pennsylvania Dispatch* had been left in the motel room Smith had rented for access to a telephone. Smith had the paper open on the bed, opened to a double-page advertisement over the center fold.

He pointed at the pages and Remo looked at them.

> AT LAST,
> WE KNOW THE CAUSE
> OF AMERICA'S PROBLEMS.

"So do I," said Remo. "Americans."

"Read it," Smith said.

Remo read the copy on the left-hand page. It was brief and direct.

America's blacks, it said, suffered from long-standing problems: high unemployment, poor educational facilities, narrow job opportunities, absorption in a culture that did not recognize their rich cultural heritage.

America's whites, the advertisement said, suffered from a growing inability to walk the streets of their towns and cities safely and a growing sense that the government in Washington was no longer interested.

"Hear, hear," said Remo.

"Read it," said Smith.

Whites felt that the products of their labor and their work was being drained from them in higher taxes, higher prices, and more government programs from which they could see no benefit.

This caused increased irritation and conflict between the races.

But now, the advertisement said, there was an answer.

Blacks wanted primarily economic and cultural security. Guaranteed jobs, shelter, food, and the opportunity to learn of their rich background, while being with people who shared that background.

Whites wanted to know that their streets were again safe and that the government's hand was not always in their wallet, taking their tax money and using it to support the same people who made the streets unsafe.

"That's right," Remo said. "We pay too much taxes."

"You haven't paid any tax in ten years," Smith said. "Except sales tax on all the junk you buy and charge to me."

"Don't knock it," said Remo. "That should be enough to run the northeast for six months."

"Read," said Smith.

A new association had been formed, the advertisement said. It was going to bring to the American public new and specific proposals to end the racial tensions and the economic problems that had racked America for the last generation.

"But to get it done, you have to stand up for us. A nationwide movement is now being formed, headquartered in the historic town of Gettysburg, Pennsylvania, and we will soon be marching on Washington.

"We hope that fifty million of you Americans will make that march with us so the government will know we mean business. This is a caravan for a new America."

It went on like that, a political call to arms.

The right-hand page was filled with signatures of people endorsing the ad.

Remo finished reading it and looked at Smith.

"So? What's it all about?"

Smith pointed at the slogan across the bottom of the page:

SAVE LIVES. AVERT VIOLENCE. ENERGIZE.

"Look at that," Smith said. "S-L-A-V-E. These people want to bring back slavery."

"And that's what's behind Bleech and his army," Remo said.

Smith was thumping a fist into a palm. As ever, his face showed no emotion, but he knew that Smith felt the emotion, the revulsion against what was planned. The notion of slavery hit at the heart of his rock-ribbed New England traditions and ancestry and background.

The right-hand page of the advertisement was small type. It included column after column of people who endorsed the ad. There were forty-seven congressmen and senators, twelve governors, and hundreds of mayors. A former Republican candidate for President. Ministers, lecturers, and writers. Three quarters of the staffs of the *Village Voice*, *Ring Magazine*, and *Better Homes and Gardens*.

"If this thing is so bad," Remo asked, "why the hell are all these names on it?"

"What do they know?" Smith said. "Most people sign these advertisements without even knowing what they say. Because someone asked them to. By the time they find out it's a call to re-institute slavery, their names will have done their work. Maybe fifty million people *will* march on Washington."

"It's your problem," Remo said. "I'm not in this kind of work anymore."

Ruby and Chiun came in from outside where they had been in deep conversation.

Ruby pointed a finger at Remo. "It's your problem, too. You promised you help me find Lucius? Did you help me find Lucius? No, you ain't helped me find Lucius. Now, you ain't done until you do. You hear?" Her voice had steadily risen in pitch, and, because it cut through Remo like a knife, he raised his hands in surrender.

"Okay, okay, okay," he said. "I'll do it. I'll do anything. Just stop yelling at me."

"Anything?" asked Chiun.

"Not that anything," said Remo. "Do you really think I could take that screeching for the rest of my life?"

"Not for the rest of your life. Just a minute or two," Chiun said. "Then it will be over and I will manage the results of it."

"What are you talking about now?" Ruby asked.

"He's talking about breeding you and me so he can have a kid to teach."

141

"Not on your life," said Ruby.

"But think," said Chiun. "Remo is white and you are brown, so a child would be tan. Now tan is not yellow, but it is closer than white or brown. That would be a start."

"You want yellow, hire yourself a Chinaman," Ruby said.

Chiun spat. "I want yellow, but not at the price of sloth or disease or treachery. I would rather have a Russian than a Chinaman."

"Then get yourself a Russian," said Ruby. "I ain't gonna do the do with him, just to make you happy."

Smith shushed them. He was on the telephone, talking slowly and smoothly into the mouthpiece.

"That's right, Chiun," said Remo. "That's the way I feel, too."

"The two of you are hopeless," said Chiun. "Anyone with half a brain could see the merits of my suggestion."

Remo fell onto the bed. "No, thank you," he said with disgust.

Ruby looked at him with curiosity.

"What you mean, talking like that?" she said.

"I'm rejecting you," Remo said.

"You not rejecting me. I rejecting you."

"We're rejecting each other," said Remo.

"No, we're not. You got nothing to say about it," Ruby said. "If I wanted you, I'd get you."

"Never."

Chiun was nodding at Ruby, patting her on the shoulder in encouragement.

"You think you're special?" she asked Remo. "I get turkeys like you any time I want."

"Not this turkey," Remo said.

"We'll see about that," Ruby said. "You willing to pay for this? You was talking about thousands of gold pieces."

"The wealth of ages," Chiun said.

"That means two bags of sea shells and fourteen dollars worth of junk jewelry," Remo said. "And twenty-two Cinzano ashtrays that he's stolen from different hotels."

"Silence," said Chiun. "This does not concern you."

"That's right, dodo. It doesn't concern you," Ruby said.

"Funny," said Remo, putting his hands behind his head. "I would've sworn it concerned me most of all."

"Ignore him, child," Chiun said.

"We'll talk about this later when he's not around," Ruby said.

Smith hung up the telephone.

"Despite all your attempts to make it impossible," he said, "I've checked it all out."

Remo looked at the ceiling tiles and began to count them.

"I was just talking to the computers at . . ." Smith paused and glanced at Ruby. "My offices," he said.

"And are they having a nice day?" Remo asked. "How's the weather up there? I hope it's not chilling their little solenoids."

Smith ignored him. He raised his left hand to rub his right shoulder where the gun butt had smashed.

"The land in the piney woods is owned by a corporation controlled by Baisley DePauw."

Remo sat up in the bed. "That's what that

143

make-believe colonel said, too, and I still don't believe it. Baisley DePauw is the left wing ding-dong liberal hoople of all time. Your computers are all wet."

"And this advertising," Smith said, "appeared in most of the daily newspapers today. It was placed by an organization funded by a foundation. The foundation is controlled by Baisley De-Pauw."

Remo lay back on the bed. "I don't believe it," he said.

"And Baisley DePauw has bought up three hours of television time on all the networks seven days from today."

"Not him," Remo said. "I don't believe it."

"The buses we saw today are owned by one of the DePauw companies," Smith said.

"I don't believe it."

"And last week, the day after the raid on Norfolk, two buses like that were seen driving into DePauw's West Palm Beach mansion," Smith said.

"I don't believe it," Remo said. "Not Baisley DePauw."

"The combined payroll costs of DePauw's companies is close to one billion dollars," Smith said. "Annually. Slavery will save him at least five-hundred million dollars a year."

"I believe it," Remo said. "A buck's a buck. Speaking of which, where is Lucius?"

"He be at the West Palm Beach house," said Ruby.

Smith nodded. "It seems that way."

"Then let's go," said Ruby.

"You go," said Remo. "I can't. My heart is broken. Dear, sweet Baisley DePauw. Slavery. From

144

the man who gave us such great stage hits as *Kill the Honkey* and *Up Against the Wall, Mother* and who's personally gone bail for every maniacal killer in this country if they're the right color. . . ."

"None of them are the right color," Chiun said. "The right color is yellow."

"I just don't believe it. You go," Remo said.

He looked at Ruby. Slowly her mouth opened. She was working herself up to screech at him. He could see it in her eyes. He clapped his hands over his ears.

But it wasn't good enough. Ruby let loose a string of curses that would have bubbled wallpaper.

"All right, all right," said Remo. "Enough. I'll go."

" 'Cause you promised," Ruby said.

Remo surrendered. "Because I promised." He looked around and his eyes fixed on Smith. "All right," Remo told Ruby. "I'll go with you, but I don't have to take him along. I don't think I could take that trip. We'll park him someplace so he can get that shoulder fixed up."

"Mama'll take care of his shoulder," Ruby promised.

CHAPTER TWELVE

The DePauw mansion overpowered the neighboring West Palm Beach mansions like a two-carat blue-white set among diamond chips.

It sat on six acres of land, surrounded on three sides by ten-foot-high white iron fencing whose bars were too close together for a human to slide between. At the back of the mansion was the Atlantic Ocean. A large powerboat, tied up to a dock, could be seen through the estate's front gate.

Inside the gate, leaning against the white brick pillars, were two uniformed guards.

Remo drove past the estate and parked a half block away. "It's probably best if you stay here," he told Ruby.

"I'm going," she said. "Case Lucius is there."

"Brave, too," Chiun said to Remo. "Not only strong and smart, but brave, too."

"I now pronounce you man and wife," Remo said. "Will you knock it off?"

"Ingrate," hissed Chiun.

Remo got out of the car and slammed the door behind him. He was halfway to the DePauw mansion when Ruby and Chiun left the rented car.

Remo was tired to death of being pushed around, tired of having his mind made up for him, tired of being told what to do and when to do it. Thank God for the Vega-Choppa. It was the first honest dollar he had earned since he stopped being a city policeman a lot of years before.

If he had not given Ruby his promise, he would keep walking right now, past the DePauw mansion, and never look back. Being pushed around. It was what had tired him of working for Smith and for CURE and he was tired of it from Chiun and tired of it from Ruby.

He stopped outside the tall white gate and motioned one of the guards to come over.

"Yes?" the guard said.

"Look. We can do this easy or we can do it hard."

"Easy? Hard?"

"Just let me in," Remo said.

"Are you expected?"

"No. But my winning ways will soon have everybody forgetting that."

"Then I'm sorry, sir, but . . ."

"Not as sorry as you will be," Remo said.

He reached through the bars of the gate, grabbed the guard's wrist and gently pulled him close. To the other guard, it looked as if the man had stepped forward so Remo could whisper something in his ear.

"Now," Remo said softly. "This is still your wrist I'm holding in my hand. We can keep it a wrist or we can make it into jelly. Take your pick."

"Wrist," the guard said.

"Good. Now call your buddy over."

"Joe," the guard called out. "Come here a minute."

"Good," said Remo. "Very good."

"Yeah, Willie," the other guard said when he reached the fence but before he could get an answer, his left wrist was in Remo's left hand.

"Now if you both don't want your ping pong careers ended for good, open the gate." He squeezed on Willie's wrist for emphasis and the guard's hand went to the ring of keys at his waist. He fumbled them loose, and used a large brass key to open the gate. It opened and Remo released both men momentarily, slid inside, then resumed his grip on their wrists. He walked them over to the high shrubbery alongside the brick pillars, transferred his grip to their necks, and left them sleeping underneath the japonica shrubs.

When he stepped back to the ceramic tiled driveway, Chiun and Ruby were entering through the gate.

"How was that?" Remo asked. "All right? Did I open the gate well enough for you two geniuses? In your wisdom, do you approve?"

Ruby looked at Chiun. "What's wrong with him now?" she asked.

"I can never figure out what white people are talking about."

"Me neither," said Ruby.

"Yeah? Yeah?" said Remo. "White people, hah? Big friends, you two, hah? Have him tell you about how God made man and put it in the oven and kept getting it wrong. Have him tell you that, you want to find out what a tolerant warm wonderful person he is."

"Ignore him," said Chiun. "He knows, better than anyone else, how tolerant I am of inferiors."

"Hah," said Remo, and walked off up the long driveway.

The main house stood at the back of the property, its rear patio extending down to the water line and the docks. There were two small buildings on one side of the house and Remo cut across the slightly overgrown lawns to go to those buildings first.

The first room must have been the gardener's quarters. There were two rooms, immaculately clean. And empty.

The second building, hidden from the street by the first building, was made of fieldstone. Remo tried to look inside, but there were curtains over the windows.

There was a hasp on the outside of the front door for padlocking the small building from the outside, but the door itself was unlocked.

The three stepped into one large room, twenty-five feet square. Thin metal bunks, covered with bare striped ticking mattresses, lined one wall. In a corner was an open toilet bowl and a sink. On another wall, chains had been installed at about the height of a man's shoulders.

Ruby counted the metal bunks. Thirteen. But fourteen men had been kidnapped.

Remo heard a sound.

"You hear it, Chiun?" he asked.

Chiun nodded.

Ruby strained but heard nothing.

"What is it?" she asked. "What do you hear?"

"Some kind of machinery whirring," Remo said.

149

He began to look around the room carefully. The sound was loudest near the wall of the building, next to the main DePauw house.

There was a ragged rug under Remo's feet. He kicked it aside and found a trap door with a large sunken ring cut into the wooden floor.

He pulled up on the ring and the trap door lifted noiselessly.

Now Ruby could heard the sound, too. It was a slow, steady whirring. She stood alongside Remo and looked down into the open well. Steep wooden stairs had been erected against the wall, and Remo led the way down.

They were in a tunnel seven feet high and not that wide. It stretched ahead of them for thirty feet and ended at a door. There was a piece of black plastic covering the door's windows on their side. Remo peeled a piece of it away and they lifted it slightly to peer in.

They saw a long conveyor belt and thirteen men standing alongside it. The first seven of them wrapped metal bands around sticks; the last six removed the metal bands and brought the sticks and bands back to the front of the line so the cycle could start over again.

All the men were black. They wore white cotton sleeveless undershirts. The room was illuminated by bare overhead bulbs.

Ruby sipped in her breath.

She started to cry out, but Remo clapped his hand over her mouth.

"What?" he said.

"That's Lucius."

"Which one?"

"The first one on the left side."

Remo watched for a moment. There seemed to be nothing to distinguish Lucius from any of the other dozen men working at the conveyor table.

At the end of the conveyor belt, on a small platform, stood a wiry man with red hair. He wore a white suit and a white hat and metal-tipped boots and carried a long whip coiled in his right hand.

On the far side of the room, six feet up the wall, there was a door, and, as the three of them watched, the door opened.

Striding out onto a raised platform that looked over the room was Baisley DePauw. Remo recognized him from the newspaper photographs. Baisley DePauw dedicating the liberation library. Baisley DePauw sending his personal jet to Algeria to bring back exiled black Americans. Baisley DePauw opening his heart and his checkbook to every crack-brained anti-American movement that had come up in Remo's remembrance.

"How are they doing?" DePauw called out to the overseer.

"All right, sir. They get faster every day," the man called back. He had a deep tomb of a voice and Remo thought it odd that for his overseer, DePauw had hired someone obviously from the streets of New York City.

"I've got another inspection today," DePauw said. "I want them singing. Slaves should sing to show how happy they are."

The whip went singing out over the men's heads, cracking sharply in empty space.

"You heard the massa. Sing."

Without slowing down their work, the slaves looked at each other.

151

"Sing, I said," the overseer shouted.

The men were still silent.

"You, Lucius. You start it."

Ruby's brother looked up and smiled a fetching grin.

"What should I sing, massa boss?"

"I don't know. Sing anything you know."

"I don't know many songs," Lucius said.

"Sing what you know. Something with a beat so you can speed up your work."

Lucius opened his mouth and the first halting words came out:

> Disco Lady.
> Will you be my baby?
> Saturday night
> to Sunday's light,
> Be my baby, Disco lady.

"Stop it," DePauw roared, just as the other men began to join in the singing.

"That's not exactly what I had in mind," De-Pauw said. "I'll have some words printed up and they can memorize them. Something inspiring, like 'All God's Chilluns Got Shoes.'"

"I'll make sure they learn it, Mr. DePauw."

DePauw nodded and went back inside through the door, which he closed tightly behind him.

"What do you think?" Remo asked Ruby.

"They're working pretty good," she said. "I might put a line like that in my wig factory. Turn up the work."

"You ought to be ashamed of yourself," Remo said.

"I won't make them sing," Ruby said.

"I don't like that disco music either," Remo said. "Anyway, Lucius looks all right."

"He looks better somehow," Ruby said.

"Maybe work agrees with him," Remo said.

"Maybe. I wouldn't know. I never saw him work before."

Through this, Chiun had been silent. Remo looked at him and saw the hazel eyes burning with an intensity that Remo had rarely seen.

"What's wrong, Chiun?"

Chiun waved a hand at the door. "This," he said. "This. It is degrading. It is evil."

Remo cocked his head. "This from the man with all the stories of how everybody is inferior to those from Sinanju?"

"It is one thing to understand men as they are, to know their weaknesses, and to deal with them thusly. It is something else to treat man as less than man. Because he who does that defies the glory of God's creation."

Just then the whip lashed again in the slave's workroom. The overseer bellowed, "Faster," and Chiun could take no more.

"Hold!" he cried and with anger fueling the power of his awesome art, he slammed a hand against the hinge side of the huge oaken door and the heavy wood panel shivered, and fell onto the floor in the room.

And like a yellow-robed wraith, Chiun whirled into the room and shouted again, "Hold, animal."

The overseer looked to him with a face torn between shock and anger.

The slaves looked up, hope on their faces, expecting a deliverer. But all they saw was a small yellow man in a yellow robe, looking like a doll,

153

whirling into the room, his eyes twisted in anger, glaring at the overseer.

The big man with the white hat and white suit and the pistol at his side, jumped down from his platform, whirled his whip over his head and lashed it out at Chiun.

Just as it reached Chiun, his practiced hand gave it a snap, to move the weighted tip into supersonic speed that created the whip's crack.

But there was no crack. Like a meat slicer, Chiun's right hand moved up alongside his head and as the whip reached him, he sliced off a neat six inches with the side of his palm.

The overseer drew back the whip again behind him, dragging it on the ground, readying an overhead slash that could slice a man's shoulder down to the bone. He brought the lash up over his head with the full power of his sinewy arm, but the lash stopped at Chiun, and then the red-haired man felt himself being pulled across the floor toward the small Oriental. He tried to let go of the whip but it was attached to his wrist with a thong. As he was being dragged, he reached to his side with his left hand to pull out his pistol.

He got the gun out, cocked it with his thumb, but never had time to pull the trigger before an almost-gentle appearing blow from an index finger pushed his lower mandible back into his spinal column with a total, terminal snap.

Chiun looked down as the final breath left the body on the floor, his eyes still glistening with intensity.

The slaves cheered and Chiun whirled toward them; his countenance so fearsome that they stopped in mid-cry and wondered for a split second if their salvation might be more fearful than their imprisonment.

Chiun hissed at them. "Remember you this. He who will not be a slave cannot be a slave. You disgust me, all of you, who outnumbered this vile thing and yet took his lashes in silence."

The men looked away as Remo and Ruby came into the glare of the high-ceiling'd room.

"Ruby," called Lucius.

"You all right?" she asked.

"Just tired," he said. "But all right."

From the corner of her eye, she saw Remo vault up to the platform leading to the door to the main house, the platform on which they had seen DePauw.

"Just wait here a little bit longer," Ruby said to Lucius. "We be right back." She hauled herself up onto the platform and followed Remo through the door he forced open. Behind her came Chiun and as he left the slave's workroom, the men gasped, because at one moment he was standing on the floor at the base of the little platform, and then an instant later, his body had lifted into the air onto the platform. And none of them had seen him jump.

The passageway ended at a solid wood and plaster wall. Ruby saw Remo look for a hidden switch to open the door, but instead Chiun put his hands against the two-by-four framing of the wall, pressed right, then left, determined that the hidden door slid left, and pushed against it with more force than seemed to exist in his frail, aged body.

There was a croaking sound as the locking

mechanism surrendered and the door panel slid smoothly to the left. They were looking into a large hallway on the main floor of the DePauw mansion.

Facing them at the end of the hall were two men. They wore neat business suits, but under the suits were the beefy bodies of athletes. They reached for their guns inside their jackets.

"Hold it right there," one of them called.

"Back in the passage," Remo told Ruby and she stepped back behind the safety of the wall.

She did not see what happened next. She heard a *whooshing* sound, and later realized it had been Chiun and Remo moving. Then she heard two faint thudding noises. There were no shots and no groans.

"All right," Remo called.

She peered around the edge of the wall. The two guards were at the end of the hallway, lying in a crumpled pile. Their hands were still inside their jackets, still reaching for their guns.

Remo answered the unspoken question in Ruby's eyes.

"Slow, slow," he said. "They were slow. And slow is the second worst sin, next to sloppy."

"He knows we're here," said Ruby.

She pointed up toward the ceiling. In the triple junction of the two walls and the ceiling was a closed circuit television camera, with a red light on under the lens. There was another at the other end of the hallway.

"Good," said Remo. "He'll have time to pray." He looked up to the camera, pointed to it as if to say "you" then put his hands in the steeple position of praying.

Behind the guards, a large curving staircase led to the mansion's second floor.

In the back of the building they found De-Pauw's suite of offices. In the outside office was a small man in a neat brown suit, with a graying crew cut, and a face that looked as if it had spent the weekend at a convention of vampire bats.

As the three came into the room, he stared at them in total horror. Ruby saw on his desk a television monitor that flashed from scene to scene from the cameras around the house. He had seen Remo and Chiun enter downstairs. He had seen the guards reach for their guns, and shout for them to stop. He had seen Ruby duck back behind the wall. But he had not seen Remo and Chiun move. He had not even seen the blur of speed. Instead, he had simply seen Chiun and Remo reappear at the other end of the hall as if by magic and he had seen the two guards drop, their hands still reaching for their guns.

"Where is he?" asked Remo.

The man was not about to argue. He pointed to a heavy wooden door.

"In there," he said. "But the door's locked from the inside. I heard Mr. DePauw bolt it."

"Yeah, right," said Remo.

As Ruby watched, Remo tossed himself at the door. He should have bounced off like a tennis ball rebounding from a brick wall. But when his shoulder hit against the door, he seemed to cling there, off his feet, pressed against the wood, and Ruby heard the ripping sound of lumber as the door broke loose and swung open smoothly.

Remo winked at her. "Don't tell anybody how I did that," he said. "It's a secret."

"A secret how he does it without denting his head," Chiun said.

DePauw's inner office was empty. But as they stepped into the room, a mechanical voice spoke out.

"Who are you? What do you want?"

"Come out, come out wherever you are," said Remo.

Chiun pointed toward a high shelf of books. The sound had come from a speaker hidden there.

Remo moved to the back windows of the office, past a desk that was filled with advertising proofs. Ruby glanced at the stack. Each ad bore the S-L-A-V-E slogan at the end and her quick glance showed clearly the design of the advertising program. It was a carefully calculated orchestration, starting with the promise of a solution to America's unrest, moving into a massive march on Washington, and ultimately to a national referendum on "Security for Blacks, Safety for Whites." Bleech's army up in Gettysburg had been trained to fight, but if DePauw's mind-bending program worked, not a shot would be fired, and Bleech's troops would merely lead fifty million people toward Washington, D.C. to force a vote on the slavery referendum.

The amplifed voice spoke again in the office. "Who are you?"

Remo gestured Chiun to the windows. Below, they could see Baisley DePauw on the back of the power boat, its motors running, a microphone in his hand.

Chiun nodded. There was a stairway leading down to the ground from the back of the office.

Remo whispered to Ruby. "You stay here and talk to him. We're going after him."

"What should I say?"

"You've never had any shortage of words before," Remo said. "Yell at him. Pretend he's me."

Chiun and Remo went back out through the front office door. Ruby realized if they went down the rear stairs, DePauw would see them and power off in the boat before they could reach him.

"We came to sign up," Ruby said aloud in the office. She was surprised how her voice echoed off the wood walls.

"Sign up for what?" DePauw answered. On the boat below, she saw DePauw looking up at the office windows and she moved toward the corner of the window so she would not be recognizable.

"The movement," she said. "It's just what we need. What gave you the idea?" Keep him talking, she thought.

"We appreciate all the support we can get. But exactly who are you?"

Ruby saw two flashes pass along the side of the house and out onto the bright sunlit lawn leading to the dock. Remo and Chiun were on the pier, and then they were leaping onto the boat.

"We're the people who gonna bury you, you crazy honkey shit," Ruby shouted in savage triumph, then flung open the window and started down the back staircase.

When she got to the dock, DePauw was sitting in a folding chair on the teakwood back deck of the boat. Chiun was casting off lines and Remo was trying to figure out how to make the boat go forward.

DePauw looked at Ruby with undisguised loathing as she lightly hopped aboard the boat.

She smiled and chucked him under the chin with a finger.

"This the way it happens," she said. "First we moves into your boat, then your neighborhood, and before you know it the whole country be shot to hell."

With a lurch, Remo finally got the boat moving forward and it spun out into the warm blue waters of the Atlantic. After five minutes of running at top speed, he cut the engines back to idle and let the boat drift gently on the small hillocks of wave water.

When he came back to the deck, DePauw had his arms folded across the chest of his natty blue pin-striped suit.

"I want to see badges," he said to Remo. "Let's start with you." He started to rise from his chair, but Remo put a hand on his shoulder and pushed him back into place.

"We don't have badges," Remo said.

"Then just who the hell do you think you are, marching onto my boat like this, taking over, holding me prisoner?"

"Is there somehow some difference between what we're doing," asked Ruby, "and what you did to those men in your cellar?"

DePauw started to respond, then closed his mouth tightly and set his jaw.

"I'll tell *you* then," Ruby said. "There's one difference. You deserve it."

"You'd better take me back before you get into real trouble."

"Sorry," said Remo. "Since you people landed

the first slaves, your family's been sucking up off America, fattening up on other people's work. Today the bill comes due."

Chiun had been staring back at the southern Florida coastline. He turned and said, "You are stupid, stupid. Sinanju, which deserves them, does not keep slaves. What therefore gives you the right?"

"Some people are fit only to be slaves," De-Pauw said. "Now that's enough talk. I want my lawyer."

"You won't need him," Remo said. "The verdict's in. For every crime that your family has ever committed against people, for two-hundred years, you're guilty. And there's no appeal of the sentence."

"That's against the law," DePauw sputtered.

"Only American law," Remo said.

DePauw looked to Chiun. The old Oriental shook his head.

"Not against Korean law," he said.

In desperation, DePauw looked to Ruby.

"Ain't against mine neither," she said. "Everybody know we lawless beasts."

In the corner of the boat, Remo ripped the anchor chain loose from its cleat, and dragged the anchor back toward DePauw who watched him in horror.

"I want a trial," DePauw said.

"You don't need one," Remo said. "You're getting justice."

He pulled DePauw to his feet. DePauw was bigger than Remo and he struggled to free himself, but Remo ignored the struggling and began wrapping the inch-thick anchor chain around his

161

body as easily as if it had been an inert lump of mud.

"You can't do this," DePauw shouted. "This is America."

"Right," Remo agreed. "Best country ever. And it'll be even better after you leave."

"I want my lawyer," DePauw screamed as Remo twisted the ends of chain together in front of DePauw's waist.

Remo stood up and met DePauw's eyes with a wink.

"Why?" he asked. "He swim better than you?"

With no more effort than it would take to dribble a basketball, Remo hauled DePauw to the edge of the boat and threw him over. There was one last scream but it turned into a gurgle as the water rushed over his plummeting body and De-Pauw vanished from sight.

"Satisfied, Ruby?" Remo asked.

She nodded. She looked down at the water where DePauw had vanished. There were a few bubbles breaking the surface, as if the life was boiling out of Baisley DePauw. And then nothing.

Remo put the boat in forward gear and spun it around, heading back toward the DePauw mansion.

As the boat roared toward land, Ruby stood alongside Chiun on the rear deck, looking out past the wake at the spot where DePauw had submerged.

"'S funny," Ruby said. "We come to this country in chains and we gets out of them and still there's always somebody trying to put those chains back on."

She looked toward Chiun, who slowly turned

his face toward her, then reached out his hand and touched her cheek.

"You need never fear," he said, before turning away. "Chains find only willing wrists."

Remo neatly solved the docking problem by letting the boat run aground on the beach behind the house. The three of them walked around the back of the main house to the front door of the building that served as the slaves' sleeping quarters.

As they went in, they heard the sound of motors.

Three Rolls Royces were coming up the driveway, parking in front of the main house.

"You two go down and let everybody go," Remo said. "I'll see what this is all about."

Remo reached the front steps of the main house just as the limousines disgorged their passengers. Six men, in neat dark suits, with highly polished shoes, carrying small expensive leather briefcases.

The backbone of America. Its forward-looking, creative-thinking businessmen.

"Hi," Remo said. "Mr. DePauw sent me to meet you. You're here for the demonstration?"

The men looked at each other with smiles. One of them, with hair that was styled to look unstyled, and fingernails that had been manicured to look as if he was not wearing nail polish, nodded to Remo. "Ready to be part of the new great American experiment," he said.

"I know Mr. DePauw wants you to be part of it," Remo said. "We all do. Won't you come this way?" He turned toward the steps, then stopped.

"Oh, you can let your drivers go. You'll be a couple of hours."

The businessmen began to give instructions to their chauffeurs when Remo broke in.

"No," he said. "Leave the cars. In case he wants to take you somewhere. Mr. DePauw will have drivers for them. There's a good sandwich shop down the block. Your men can kill time there until we send for them."

The businessmen gave instructions and followed Remo inside the house. He hustled them down the corridor to the left, toward the secret panel in the wall.

"Wait'll you see this," he said with a chuckle in his voice. "I know you're going to get a hoot out of it."

Ruby and Chiun had released the leg chains on the thirteen men and led them up the steps into the small slave shack. The men were looking for their clothing when Ruby heard Remo's voice coming through the open trap door from down in the work area.

"That's it," she heard him say. "You three wrap those things around and you three unwrap them. Got it?"

There was a pause and Remo's voice was louder.

"I don't hear you. You got it?"

Six voices answered in unison. "Yes sir."

"That's better," Remo said. "Now remember, Mr. DePauw wants you to be happy. And so do I. So you sing, just to show how happy you are. You know any songs?"

Again there was a silence.

164

"Any kind of song," Remo's voice said, and it was harsh and demanding.

Instantly, one frail nasal voice began to sing tentatively.

"Good," Remo said. "Now louder. And all of you join in.

The voices came now, recognizable.

Disco Lady.
Won't you be my baby?

Ruby laughed aloud. Remo's voice again: "Thattaway. Now just keep working there and don't worry about a thing. Somebody'll be along and get you out of those leg irons. Probably no more than a couple of days."

A minute later, Remo came up through the trap door into the shack.

The black men were dressing. They looked at Remo as he came in. He met their eyes, then jerked his thumb over his shoulder toward the trap door.

"You've all been replaced."

One of the black men cocked an ear to listen to the weak strings of "Disco Lady."

"Gotta admit it," he said. "Them white folks sure's got rhythm. Makes you want to tap yo' feet and dance."

Remo told them they were driving home to Norfolk in style. "Take the Rolls Royces in front. Nobody's going to miss them for awhile."

The black men ran toward the front of the shack, Lucius Jackson among them.

"Hey, Lucius," Ruby called. "You gonna go back with us?"

"Hell, no," Lucius called over his shoulder. "I wanna ride in that Rolls Royce."

Ruby turned to Remo as her brother went outside into the sunlight. "I think I liked him better when he was wrapping that metal around those poles."

CHAPTER THIRTEEN

Their car was the first back to Norfolk and Ruby led Remo and Chiun upstairs to give her mother the good news.

"Mama, Lucius is coming home," Ruby said.

Her mother inhaled a deep lungful of pipe and exhaled a smoke that looked greenish. She looked down at her feet.

"What he been doin' the last week?" she asked.

"Working," Ruby said.

Her mother looked up at her sharply.

"You sure it be Lucius?"

For the first time, she seemed to notice Remo and Chiun. "That fella you be leavin' here, I fix up his arm best I could. But then he wen' over the hotel to stay. Say?"

"Say what?" said Remo.

"Iffen he be a doctor, how come he cain't fix his own arm?"

"Not that kind of a doctor."

Mrs. Gonzalez nodded, her dark face deepened with chasms of crease wrinkles. "Guess not. Otherwise he be able to fix hisself up."

"Where is he?" said Remo.

"De hotel."

"Which one?"

"One of dem."

Remo looked around to Ruby for help. She was talking agitatedly with Chiun in a corner of the room.

"Ruby," Remo squawked.

"He's at the Holiday Inn," she said. "You two can go ahead. I'll meet you there. I want to make sure Mama's all right."

Smith was sitting in his hotel room in a straight backed chair, reading newspapers. The room looked as if it had emerged from the hermetically sealed pages of a Sears Roebuck catalogue, as if no one alive had ever been in it, and looking at Smith's pinched acid face, Remo saw no reason to dispute that judgment.

"How's the shoulder?" Remo said.

"I think by tomorrow I will have been able to wash off all that green slime that woman insisted on putting on it. Then I won't be too embarrassed to go to a doctor."

Chiun opened Smith's shirt and pulled it down off his right shoulder to investigate the wound. He pressed with his fingers and nodded.

"That green slime has done very nicely," he said. "I must learn what it was. You are healing well."

"What happened in Florida?" Smith said, rebuttoning his shirt.

Remo found it hard to remember the last time he had seen Smith without a jacket and vest.

"Florida?" Smith repeated.

"Oh, yeah," Remo said. "DePauw is dead. The prisoners are free. God's in his heaven, all's right with the world, and I'm back in retirement."

"Well, perhaps," said Smith. "But there's one thing left."

Remo's face was grim as he leaned toward Smith.

"As long as I've known you, Smitty, there's always been just one more thing."

"Listen to the emperor, Remo," said Chiun, "who knows but that this one more thing may yet bring glory to your dull life. Tell him, Emperor, tell him. What is this one more wondrous thing?"

Smith cleared his throat. "Yes, well. You know that we can operate only in secrecy. Without secrecy, CURE goes under."

"I've heard that and heard it and heard it," Remo said.

"Our secrecy has been breached. Shattered, I guess, is more accurate."

"Good. Then go out of business. Open a dry goods store someplace up in New Hampshire. Cheat the locals before they cheat you. I know a good real estate agent. If you like houses without roofs."

Chiun looked stern. "Remo, since you have been on television, you have lost all your manners. Is that what being a star has done to you? Show respect for the little people."

"Who are the little people, Chiun?"

"Everybody but me."

"All right, Smitty, I'll hear you out before I laugh in your face. Who breached security this time? And so what?"

"Ruby Gonzalez," Smith said. "And you've got to dispose of her."

Smith watched closely. Remo's face showed no emotion. He simply stood back from Smith's chair and looked out a window. "Why don't we talk English, Smitty? You don't mean dispose of her, you mean kill her, don't you?"

"All right, kill her."

"Stuff it. You forgot that I quit."

"Just this one more thing."

"Never again. I'm retired. You want her hit, talk to Chiun. He's still in the business. But I won't."

Smith looked at Chiun who shook his head sadly. "Any enemy of yours, Emperor, is an enemy of mine. Point them out and they will feel the wrath of Sinanju. But not that girl with the Brussels-sprout ears. Not her."

"Why is she different?"

"She is going to give me a son. It is all arranged."

"You? A son?"

"It will technically be Remo's, of course," Chiun said.

"I have something to say about this," Remo said without turning.

Behind his back, Chiun shook his head, indicating to Smith that Remo would have nothing to say about it at all.

"So this I cannot do," Chiun said. "Not by my hand can I lose the only good recruit my House will ever have, my chance, like all the other Masters for centuries, to pass on my secrets to someone deserving."

Remo sniffed his disgust.

"Guess you'll have to do it yourself," he said. "Get a taste of what it's like."

"I guess I will," Smith said.

"You do that." He winked at Chiun who turned his back so Smith would not see him smile.

"I will," said Smith.

There was a knock at the door.

"It's open," Remo called.

Ruby stepped in. She had changed to a sleeveless white dress. Her skin looked as smooth and pure as melted maple ice cream. Her face shone with the young look of a woman who found all the cosmetic help she needed in a bar of soap.

"Hello," she said to Smith. She nodded to Remo and Chiun. "They told you what happened?"

Before Smith could answer, Remo said "No. We never tell him. We just tell him it's taken care of. He doesn't like to hear details because then he might, just might, realize once, just once, that somebody dies every time we make a new corpse for him. He doesn't want to hear about that. He just wants us to send him monthly lists of victims for his statistical charts."

"Gotta have charts," Ruby said mildly.

"Then you talk to him," Remo said. "He's got some business with you anyway. Chiun and I are going next door. You talk with him."

In the next room, as the door closed behind him, Remo asked Chiun, "How long?"

"What is this how long?" said Chiun.

"How long will it take for her to con him out of his socks?"

"How long do you say?" asked Chiun.

"Five minutes," said Remo.

"Three," said Chiun.

"You're on. Nobody can con Smith in three minutes. My own personal record is five minutes fifteen."

"What are we wagering?" asked Chiun.

"Anything you want, Little Father."

"Anything?"

"Anything except that," Remo said.

In the next room, Ruby sat in a chair facing Smith, who drummed his fingertips on the small blond formica desk.

Finally Ruby broke the silence. "How you gonna do it?"

"Excuse me?"

"You. How you gonna do it? A gun or what?"

Smith sat back in his chair. "How do you know that?"

"It's not hard. You're the brains of this here operation. It's what I'd do if it came to it."

"Oh, I see," said Smith. He had never had anyone offer himself up for killing before.

"Course it might not be in your best interests," said Ruby.

"Perhaps you'd tell me why."

"Sure. Since't I came here and I knew what you were fixin' to do, I'd be kind of a dope to just walk in and let it go like that. So I took precautions."

"What kind of precautions?"

"I wrote down everything I know and I spread it around a bit."

"I've heard that many times before," Smith said.

"Yeah, I know. Somebody's always giving something to their lawyer for when they die and like that. And then you get to the lawyer first so nothing happens. Well, I didn't do that. I left everything where the CIA gets it if I die."

Smith looked at Ruby with narrowed eyes.

She nodded.

"I figured you can maybe get to my lawyer or something, maybe make sure that what I tell him don't get out. But the CIA? They gonna have a field day when they find out what you doing when they been getting their ears pinned back for less. They never let up on you. CURE goes right down the drain."

Smith sighed and Ruby said, "Now look at the good side."

"There is no good side."

"Sure, there is. First you think I know a little bit about your organization, enough to be dangerous. And that's only part right. I know a whole lot about your organization."

"How'd you learn that?"

She jerked a thumb over her shoulder. "I been with them on two separate things now. You have to be deaf, dumb, and blind not to find things out. I know who you are and where you operate and what you do and what you do personally and what they do and I have an idea of what you spend and where the President keeps the phone he calls you on and what your telephone codes are. Like that. Ceppin' for you, I guess I know more about your operation than anybody in the world."

"Just what I needed," Smith said. "A woman who knows too much that I can't get rid of."

"Want me to tell you what to do?" asked Ruby.

"What?"

"Hire me."

"Hire you? What for?"

"Nothing special. Not right now. But I hear

things. I keep track of things. Sometimes you need special help, you call me. I smart and I don't say nothin' to nobody."

"Do I have a choice?"

"No. That's why this is your lucky day," said Ruby.

"How much do you want?"

"Make me an offer."

"Five thousand dollars."

"You fooling," Ruby said.

"Why?"

"I making twenty-five with the CIA before I left."

"For what?" asked Smith. His first salary with the CIA had been seven thousand dollars a year, but that was long ago.

"For hanging around. In three years, they call me once. They send me down to that island and I run into those two inside there. I helped you then and when I got back, I didn't go running around, telling everybody I was a big spy, helping a big secret organization."

"I'll give you twenty-three," said Smith, surrendering.

"Thirty," said Ruby.

"Split the difference. Twenty-five," said Smith.

"Splittin' the difference is twenty-six five."

"All right," Smith said, swallowing hard. "But it's banditry."

"Yeah. But now I be your bandit. And I'm gonna earn my money for you in less than five minutes."

She left Smith with a puzzled look on his face and opened the door to the other room.

"Why'nt you come in?"

174

Chiun smiled at Remo triumphantly. "Two minutes and fifty-five seconds. You owe me."

"*Aaah*," said Remo in disgust. "Don't worry. I'll pay you. As soon as I get my residual check from Vega-Choppa."

He walked away, but as he moved, Chiun's hands flicked into Remo's pocket and came out with a roll of bills. Chiun extricated the ten dollars Remo owed him, and tossed the rest of the money onto the sofa.

Inside, Remo told Smith, "Not so easy when you've got to see their eyes, is it?"

"You're wrong, Remo. It was a simple administrative decision."

"Here's another simple administrative decision. I quit."

Smith nodded his head. "I know. What are you going to do?"

"I told you. I'm going to get a lot of residuals from those commercials for my hands. I'm going to be rich. My hands are going to be famous. Then, who knows? Maybe next my feet. Maybe they'll want somebody to do something with his feet."

"Like a monkey," said Chiun. "They do things with their feet."

"What was the name of that gadget you advertised?" asked Smith, reaching for a newspaper from the desk.

"The Vega-Choppa," said Remo.

Smith looked at the newspaper. "I don't think you'd better count on them to support you," he said.

"Why not? Let me see that."

He glanced at the story that Smith had circled.

Twenty-seven lawsuits, totaling over forty-five million dollars, had been filed against the Vega-Choppa manufacturer by housewives whose fingers and hands had been mangled using the device. They charged that the television commercials showing the product's ease of operation were misleading and had obviously been filmed at slow speed and then speeded up.

When the manufacturer denied this, the attorneys representing the injured women amended their complaints to include among the defendants a John Doe, who was the demonstrator of the device. They accused him of using manual dexterity to give housewives "a false sense of security that the utensil was safe for normal human beings to use."

Remo looked at Smith and, if he had been smiling, Remo might have killed him then and there. But Smith was as somber as usual.

"Let's see, Remo. Your share of forty-five million dollars in damages should come to twenty-two point five million. You're going to have to sell a lot of carrot cutters to make up for that."

Remo sighed. "I'll find some other work."

Ruby tapped him on the shoulder. "Could I talk to you please?"

"Talk," said Remo.

"Inside," Ruby said.

In the other room, he said "What do you want?"

"Don't be so grouchy."

"It's easy for you to say. You never just lost your chance to be a rich television star."

"You'll get another chance someday."

176

"Now what am I gonna do?" Remo asked.

"I don't care what you do," Ruby said. "I want to talk about what you did."

"Which was?"

"Freeing Lucius. Those other men."

"A favor to you. I owed you one."

"No, it wasn't. It was a duty to your country," Ruby said. "That was a good thing you did."

Remo sat heavily on the edge of the bed. He was silent for a moment before looking up.

"You really think so?"

Ruby nodded.

"It was a good thing. Today you made America a better place to live in. We should all have the chance to do that sometimes."

"You really think that, don't you? Really."

"I really do. I'm proud to know you."

Remo stood up. "You know, you're right. Getting rid of that creep today was worth a lot. It takes away a lot of the stench."

"It was a good thing," Ruby said again.

Remo took her hands. "You know, maybe Chiun's onto something. About me and you," he said.

Ruby smiled. "We'll just have to see about that."

"We will," Remo said. "We will."

He walked back into the main room of the hotel suite. Ruby followed closely behind him.

Chiun looked past Remo at her. She held up her fingers to make an okay ring.

As she passed Chiun, she leaned over and whispered, "You lose. He was easy. Where's my ten dollars?"

177

Chiun handed her the ten dollars he had filched from Remo's pocket.

Ruby tucked it into her dress and she and Chiun watched as Remo approached Smith.

"Smitty," said Remo. "I've decided to give you another chance."

Smith almost smiled.

"But if you blow this one, that's it. Right, Chiun?"

"For the first time," Chiun said.

"Right, Ruby?"

"Anything you say. Dodo."

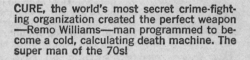

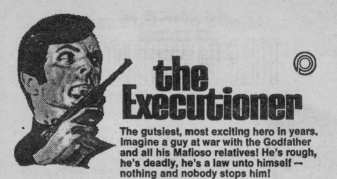

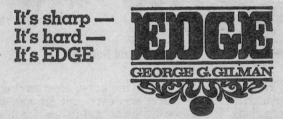

THE PENETRATOR

by Lionel Derrick

Mark Hardin. Discharged from the army, after service in Vietnam. His military career was over. But *his* war was just beginning. His reason for living and reason for dying became the same—to stamp out crime and corruption wherever he finds it. He is deadly; he is unpredictable; and he is dedicated. He is The Penetrator!

Read all of him in: